A Box of Stars Beneath the Bed

A collection of flash-fictions

Edited by
Calum Kerr, Nuala Ní Chonchúir
with Santino Prinzi

A National Flash-Fiction Day and Gumbo Press publication

First Published 2016 by National Flash-Fiction Day
in association with Gumbo Press
with support from Arts Council England

National Flash-Fiction Day
18 Caxton Avenue
Bitterne
Southampton
SO19 5LJ
www.nationalflashfictionday.co.uk

All work ©2016 the authors, unless stated otherwise.
Cover Design ©2016 Calum Kerr.

The moral right of the authors has been asserted.

All rights reserved. No part of this publication may be
reproduced, stored in a retrieval system, or transmitted,
in any form or by any means, electronic, mechanical,
photocopying, recording or otherwise, without the
prior permission of the publishers.

A CIP Catalogue record for this book
is available from the British Library

ISBN 978-1534712683

Dedicated to you,
the readers:
all of you Stars.

Contents

Foreword	The Editors	8
Before the Sun Comes Up	Tim Stevenson	11
Miss Scarlet in the Shed	Tracy Fells	13
Cold Hands	Rhoda Greaves	14
Ambush	Richard Holt	16
Outsider	Laura Huntley	18
Theseus in Belleville	Anne E. Weisgerber	20
Bocca Baciata	Ruth McKee	21
Health and Pleasure, Glorious Sea!	Sharon Telfer	22
Gingerbread	Virginia Moffatt	24
A Marionettist's Musings While on a Park Bench	Charley Karchin	26
Bubblegum Barbie	Emily Devane	27
Lifer	Adam Trodd	29
Shirts – A Fable	R.J. Dent	30
Sam, 29	Martha Gleeson	32
Three Kids, Two Balloons	K.M. Elkes	33
Who? What?	Ashley Chantler	35
Pub Quiz	Alison Wassell	36
Sushi and Kitty Cats	Kaitlyn Johnson	38
Desert Blossom	Annie Evett	40
Premiums	Ian Shine	42
Misunderstanding	Vivien Jones	43
Wakes Week	David Hartley	45
Burning Faith	Frankie McMillan	46
Pigeon English	David Cook	48
Kittiwakes	Catherine Edmunds	49
The Door Closes	Kevlin Henney	51
Clippers	Debbi Voisey	53
I Go on the Morrow to Murder the King	Joy Myerscough	54
Special Delivery	Calum Kerr	55
Grains	Joanna Campbell	57
Panda	Fat Roland	59
Fish Supper	Laura Tickle	61
The Vineyard	Catherine McNamara	62

The Pleasure Principle	Rob Walton	64
Onion	Damhnait Monaghan	66
My Aunt Maggie	Paul McVeigh	67
A Box of Stars Beneath the Bed	Jon Stubbington	69
A Collection	Diane Simmons	71
Kelly Loves Traffic Light Jelly	Jeanette Sheppard	72
Yellow	Nuala Ní Chonchúir	74
424 Likes	Jennifer Harvey	76
Manspreading	Marie Gethins	78
Wake Up	Oli Morriss	79
When Dreams are Large and Tusked	Ingrid Jendrzejewski	81
Ten Things that Happened After My Funeral	Santino Prinzi	82
What the Therapist Said	Jude Higgins	84
Gregor Samsa Quits the Track Team	Beverly C. Lucey	85
Honesty's Not the Best Policy	Brendan Way	87
Orphans	Chris Stanley	88
And the Red Flower	Nina Lindmark Lie	90
One Last Pickup	Sarah Hilary	91
Sunday Morning	John Holland	93
About Unemployment and Rats	Bernard O'Rourke	95
Captain Strix	Zoe Gilbert	96
Latchkey	Fiona J. Mackintosh	98
Lips	Nik Perring	99
Map Reading	Jane Roberts	101
How to Make Lolo	Michelle Elvy	102
Family Values	Jonathan Pinnock	104
Blackbird Singing in the Dead of Night	Claire Fuller	105
Hornet's Nest	Sally Burnette	106
The Taste of Sock and Rubber	Cathy Bryant	108
In the Café	Sherri Turner	110
On the Invisibility of the Deaf	Debbie Young	111
Flying Ant Day	Judy Darley	113
Marzipan Bride and Groom	Sal Page	114
I Believe in You	Meg Pokrass	116
When She Was Good	Safia Moore	118
Injuries in Dust	Poppy O'Neill	119
We Can Be Asteroids	F.J. Morris	121
Purple with a Purpose	Amanda Saint	123

| Little Ghosts | Jan Carson | 124 |
| The Night Life of Wives | Angela Readman | 125 |

National Flash-Fiction Day 2016
Micro-Fiction Competition Winners

The Jumper	Anne Patterson	127
A One-Word Yet...	Ingrid Jendrzejewski	128
Storm	Gemma Govier	129
Jessie Learns How to Keep A Secret	Alison Wassell	130
Illumination	Judi Walsh	131
When Words Aren't Enough	Lucy Welch	131
Christmas	James Watkins	132
Always One	Tracy Fells	132
Notes	Elaine Marie McKay	133
Energy Efficient, Extremely Slim,		
Easy to Install	Ed Broom	133

| Author Information | 134 |
| Acknowledgements | 136 |

Foreword

This year sees the fifth National Flash-Fiction Day and so the fifth anthology produced in its celebration.

We have worked hard and done our best to select what we see as the very finest stories. It's always a difficult task, made all the harder this year by a bumper crop of submissions— nearly 500 of them! —but at the end there is an immense satisfaction when the anthology comes together.

Once again, as well as the submitted pieces, we have a selection of stories commissioned from some of the 'stars' of flash-fiction, as well as some new, up-and-coming names, and all of those are rounded out with the ten winners of our micro-fiction competition. The result is a truly exceptional anthology.

As we have been putting the finishing touches to the collection, the selected title—taken from Jon Stubbington's story—has seemed more and more apt. For this is truly a box chock full of stars, each once shining its own particular light.

We have a range which runs from horror and darkness, though to humour, love and light. We have some stories which required the full 500 words to reveal themselves, and some which needed a lot less (in one case, just the one, very appropriate word). As a representation of the current state of flash-fiction it is a collection which shows the form to be in very rude health.

Thanks as ever must go out to all the writers who support NFFD every year, and to those who work so hard behind the scenes to make it happen.

Who would have thought, back in 2012, when the very first day happened, that we would be back in 2016 for our fifth? It is a real testament to the community which has grown up around NFFD, and our thanks go out to you all.

With that said, it's time for you to sit back, relax, reach under the bed for the box, look inside and see what's out there.

Calum Kerr & Nuala Ní Chonchúir
Editors
June 2016

Before the Sun Comes Up
Tim Stevenson

We were star gazing, Johnny and me, under silver blankets with a thermos of coffee, squinting through his dad's old telescope. Above us an arc of stars reached across the horizon, a billion, Johnny said, tens of billions, some with names but most without, in one galaxy of billions, stretched out in the night, forever.

"It's a ceiling," Johnny said. "It's like the ceiling to a cathedral for science." Then he stopped and laughed to himself, said something I didn't understand about faith, and laughed again.

My phone had died half an hour ago, so I stared up and listened to him talk. I worried if my sister was alright, worried I'd missed all the gossip, but the stars were nice and all, even though the coffee was cold, and I wasn't really dressed for looking through telescopes.

I thought Johnny liked me, and that's why he'd asked. Stars had sounded romantic and that when he'd said about going out, but that was when the sun was shining and I was only half paying attention anyway cos of the photos Geena had posted of her new haircut.

I wish I was wearing tights.

Johnny pulled my blanket away to put his arm around me. This is what I'd thought would happen. I didn't mind, a snog under the stars, then maybe into his car, but instead he pulled me forward and got me to look into the end of the telescope.

"Jupiter," he said.

"Whatever," I thought. I wasn't thinking about Johnny then, I was thinking about Barry. Barry had a job, and was more together, and had better clothes.

Johnny had a look himself. I could see him smiling.

"All these stars," he said, "and I end up looking at a gas giant, a big ball of fog and ice."

"Should have been Saturn," I said. "The bloke that does the horoscopes said Saturn has rings, great big ones, and deep in the middle of all that gas is a sodding great diamond. Someone must really love Saturn to give it a ring like that."

Johnny stared at me for a long time.

"That bloke was right," he said, "what other stuff did you learn from the horoscopes?"

I couldn't decide if he was serious or not so I told him anyway.

"Taurus is going to have money troubles, Cancer will get the job they want, and Pisces will have a surprise in store."

"And what sign are you?"

"I'm an Aries," I said. "Didn't say nothing about being in a field freezing my arse off."

Johnny laughed again and came in for the kiss, and about bloody time too.

While Johnny keeps me warm I can't help but think about lucky Saturn and her diamond ring. I look up at all the billions of stars, some with names, and some without, and I wonder if Johnny will ever get around to asking me mine.

Miss Scarlet in the Shed
Tracy Fells

'They're all on drugs.' My neighbour's nasal voice is clipped and posing like a show-ring poodle. The Colonel and Mrs Peacock spot me over the fence. 'Maggie,' he calls to me, moustache quivering, 'see what the brutes have done.'

Someone has beheaded his roses. Crimson petals from prize-winning blooms escape on the summer breeze clinging to their papa's mustard tank top, like bloodstains at the crime scene. He's not really a colonel, but he makes me think of that board game, where Professor Plum did it in the library with the candlestick. His wife, with auburn hair tightly restrained by an army of pins, is the prim Mrs Peacock to his blustering soldier. Later Mrs Peacock is pruning alone. She waves the secateurs in greeting. Her trug basket swings with rosebuds, still furled, inert Geisha virgins wrapped in lemon silk. Clearly the Colonel has been a naughty boy and this horticultural castration is his punishment.

The next morning I keep my head down in the bushes. The reverent hymn of lavender besotted bees dull my thoughts, yet other sounds clamour for attention. There is someone in the Colonel's potting shed. I hear the low climatic moans of a woman. She is not alone. Who is the old dog rooting in the shed?

Following the sun I tackle the honeysuckle choking the front porch. Dazed with destruction I barely register the arrival of the Colonel's Mercedes crunching into the adjacent drive. His wife erupts from the house. Hair unpinned, tumbling over bare shoulders, glinting like polished copper flecked with gold. A feline smile lingers on moist lips as she escorts out her guest. Brushing a clump of potting compost from her emerald dress another woman steps onto the gravel path.

I must rename Mrs Peacock, now her true colours are showing.

Cold Hands
Rhoda Greaves

I wasn't supposed to know where to find you. But how could you not go straight to your poor mother's arms. I waited till ten o'clock when they unlocked the gates, then snuck a peek at you. You were thinner, but that was expected. The too-big jumper I bought you for Christmas one year, now faded and bagging out of shape.

They phoned and told me, standard practice apparently. I'd only waited three years for the call. You'd been rehabilitated they said, paid your debt to society. I took a bunch of pansies when I went to tell my Rebecca. A trowel too, so I could dig out the weeds. I knew it was you, before they'd caught up with you for questioning. The way you'd put your halting hand upon her arm mid-sentence, your palm closing over her fingers as she'd reach out to take an extra slice of pizza, just one more chocolate from the box.

'God, look at that, Mum,' she'd say to me, pinching imaginary fat from her stomach. Then she'd look to you, and you'd smile at her, your eyes, all the time, layering doubt.

She would have fought you, they said, even as you crushed her larynx. Even as her hyoid bone fractured, then snapped, under the very weight of your grip. She'd won medals for synchronised swimming, could hold onto her breath for longer than most. She would have hit and scratched and thrashed and jerked – dyspnea, or the less poetic *air hunger* eventually dragging her down.

I'm outside now: that house you think you're safe in. The key you've forgotten you ever gave her, tightly wrapped in my fist. I peer through the lounge window and you're laughing at the telly. Laughing like a kid who's just got the joke. You lift a bottle of beer to your lips and allow the cold liquid to fill your throat, exposing the sharp curve of your Adam's apple.

Round the back, your mother is frying bacon, while fresh

coffee brews on the worktop, next to a bag of muffins; Tesco's finest. They'd said the cancer would get her before the first year of your sentence was up.

As I watch her – turning sausages, pouring orange juice, cracking eggs and taking two hot plates from the oven – something swoops a dive in my stomach, and my hands are forced to reach for the steadying bricks. Soon, they will find their way into open coat pockets and bury themselves deeply in fluff and used tissues. And as I turn away into the darkness, I'll hear a low humming coming from the kitchen, and if I linger for maybe just a second, will just about make out the first notes of a tune.

Ambush
Richard Holt

after the trouble the boys take to the hills for a licking of wounds and some blarney for theres stories out of exploits and in the hills stories grow big like school yarns therell be whiskey to be had and good times which is what a band o fellows wants more even than women true enough a fellow wants a yarn and whiskey and Dan will do a song and a jig and the world will be like the Lord made it sun shining bright on his creation Stevie Boy sends a message sure that's for me and I drops me shears and leaves with Cuttler cursing cause his sheeps half clipped and I take his pony for wages and goes up I'd not be missing the fun and the boys are havin a fair old time and soon enough I has a bottle and a full pipe and I's leaning back with them the sun is warm and it makes the whiskey smooth and sure enough the airs filling with singing ballads and the crows joining in and nothing in the worlds as good as that then theres a shot from the bushes and next moment all hell and the clearings got troopers and dogs have crept up on us and us only drinking and singing of lasses Joe takes a pellet but hes up and the rest are up quick smart and their rifles loaded too like they been waiting and next moment its shots near me head and Dannys rifle smoking and the two big coppers go down as quick as it started the other is high tailing and Eddy grabs at me arm and we give the dog chase he calls to the others to head off north where weve got a place and we get to our horses just as the yellow cowards mounting and we're after him and hes got no chance not with Eddy giving chase whos the best horseman and an easy match for a fat Scot at the bottom of the spur Eddys got him bail'd up I gets alongside his pistols drawn and the copper is near shittin and Eddy stares him then he spits like hes swallowed a fly and he cocks his pistol the Scot pleads like a girl to a fellow and he says if hes shot theres others will come and Eddy says I aint never shot a dog wasnt lame and the Scot looks worried then Eddy aims at his leg but instead o shooting he says you tell them others and you tell them good it was me that shot them two up there dyou understand and the dog nods and Eddy says in defence of life and limb and God is witness that's the truth and you tell it good then he takes the scoundrels gun and his horse and kicks him down the hill and we turn and head north and Eddy says to me its bad times coming

Outsider
Laura Huntley

He isn't like the others: he's quietly restrained for a zombie; no pitiful, pained, low groans escape his lips. He's a solitary creature and dines alone. The others don't notice him. Or much else. He's the odd one out. He can't quite recall but, somewhere in the recesses of his compromised and diseased mind, he suspects that he was in life. Though that is something of a blur. A fog. Occasionally, fragments knit themselves together in muddled, silent flashbacks. They play, out of sequence, in stolen glimpses and scratchy snatches; much like watching a brief black and white movie in his head. Like the old Charlie Chaplin films. But these scenes aren't funny.

He spots a young woman, in the distance, ambling towards him. The streetlights intermittently illuminate her face and long, flowing fair hair. The breeze catches her appealing jasmine-scented perfume and, suddenly, he's ravenous. His stiff body lurches into the shadows. He watches her, admiring the way that she walks. She isn't in a sleep-walking style trance, like his kind. She's human.

She's almost beside him, unaware of his presence. And that her life, as she knows it, is soon to be over; changed forever. Her floral fragrance is thick in his nostrils now and he reaches out and grabs her by the neck. She screams hysterically as he greedily bites into the tender flesh, ripping away the skin of her shoulder. Her shrieks beg for mercy. But he isn't listening. She cries out in agony, with futile fighting fists, as his fiercely-strong hands tear open her stomach and chest, and he scoops out her organs with a skilled ease. Undigested remnants of a meal linger inside of her. Steak. Well-cooked cow. It sends him into a frenzy. He slashes open her scalp, blood splatters her golden locks and the grey pavement underneath. He reaches inside and pulls out a chunk of her brain. And she's dead.

His teeth chew her grey matter. She tastes pleasingly

intelligent and well-educated. A lot don't. A lot of them taste of wasted breath and crushing disappointment. A fleeting recollection, belonging to the young lady, forms in his mind, and he pauses. He sees her as a child upon a swing; chubby, little, grazed legs dangling and kicking out.

"Higher, Daddy, higher," she demands between fits of giggles.

He spits out the rest of her brain from his mouth, choking, unable to process the new surge of feelings he's experiencing. He consumes her heart, so still now it has ceased beating. She tastes pure. He can taste her integrity and sweet nature. He isn't hungry anymore. He crawls away, retreating into the darkness and he waits.

There it is. The twitch. Her body jerks as the unstoppable venom of his bite takes over. Slowly, she pulls herself to her clumsy feet. Her eyes are vacant and she hasn't noticed the bloody state she's in. She merely wanders off, back in the direction that she'd been originally travelling. And he follows her.

Theseus in Belleville

Anne E. Weisgerber

When I saw you I saw you with laser-beam sight as I left Empenadas by Stella still singing; I sang my girl's name and I knew all my light was projected in open-faced stance, as one sinning. Her car coat swung in as I opened her door; my right hand slipped smoothly along her warm waist, unspooling her laughter, my hand finding more, I could sense you were passing, my tongue knew your taste and I thought about standing and stammering saying *but she is so warm and so firm and so willing*. A true son of Belleville, a Belleville worth slaying, whose gold in the palm runs unmelted and chilling; a moment a minute I feign an excuse, my tongue all a-tumble, unthreaded as Theseus now tired of treading your labyrinth life that reduced me to eyes seeing *only the clew*, to New York, to your bed, via more royal tread do I hear the train hear the train hear the train take you but you left behind you those shining steel threads that were caught in the caught in the stairs' endless climb. I will pin down your pines, then, Oh Minna: I'll break you.

Bocca Baciata
(after Fanny Cornforth and Dante Gabriel Rossetti)
Ruth McKee

Let in a slit of light to your mouth, pout.
He angled my face, his hands on my back, my breasts; he
wanted them cold, but my lips incarnadine.
Mystery in the face, aroused but unknowing.
I held a wand of willow, or the neck of a lyre.
Put your fingers around it, like it palpitates.
Sometimes I had to bend, as if plucking flowers.
Sumptuous amid near blooded roses, as *Venus Verticordia:* what
girl could resist?

He had plucked me too, from my father's smithy, the
church bells of metal, wildness of horse-smell. He had the
name of an angel but changed mine to suit himself.

He had me as I posed, legs apart, knees aching, the smell of
turpentine and his sweat. He painted me then, in voluptuous
heat. After, he put his fingers inside me til I groaned, then he'd
touch up the canvass and retire.

Later, when my flesh was heavy and belly full with the sin
of it, I saw the finished painting, recognized all the glory of my
thighs, my breasts, my shoulder.

But it was not my face. It was the new girl, a fresh palette
of tastes, whose lips were a near replica of mine, but her dusky
upper lip a deeper bow.

When I got pheasant fat, my face soured, he made me keep
house. I cleaned the steps as the fresh model traipsed up, her
hair aflame, his fingers poised. He didn't want a slit in my
mouth any more.
You never keep it shut.
I took a man then, and was found, sprawled, saline
mouthed and eager. *Libidinous, unruly, irrational.*
Once it was carmine, canary, and silks. Now I wear a black
dress with a white crooked collar.
It's what they wear here, at the asylum.

Health and Pleasure, Glorious Sea!
Sharon Telfer

When had she last been truly naked? She could not remember. Miss Miller blushed even to think the word. In the nursery, she thought. Below her, the waves hushed and sifted.

It seemed an impossibility, to be standing here, her white body facing her black dress in the half-light. The wooden walls creaked like stays. Without her scaffold of bodice, petticoat, corset, she feared she would collapse. So many days of packing-cases and hessian had left her powdered with dust like a moth's wing. Her modest trunks and bandboxes despatched to her new home with Aunt Marlowe. The weeks before spent stripping The Cedars, hauling down heavy velvet with Betty and Susan, beating carpets, sorting furniture for sale. Papa, first to be parcelled away in his box of gleaming mahogany, still a presence like cobwebs she could not reach.

She pulled on her costume. Could she step outside in such a manner, her legs standing out like coarse sticks? But Aunt Marlowe had insisted on it: nothing surpassed sea bathing for the nerves. And all her life, Miss Miller had done as she was told. The door was so swollen in its frame, she must put her weight to it, tottering as it swung open, one hand up against the brilliant sun.

She descended with care, the ladder trembling at the incessant rub of waves. Sand rasped her ankles, seeped between her sinking toes. She could not stand still. She must choose either to retreat or go into the sea.

The swell rolled up, then away, wrapping close round her calves, thighs, waist, and then retreating, tugging the heavy cotton back. She calmed herself, counting, steady, one, two, three, four...

When the breaker smacked her, she went under. The current whipped her like seaweed. Her hands scrabbled without purchase. She could hear nothing, see nothing, say nothing.

When the undertow let her go, she found herself facing the horizon, bathing cap gone, her hair a long, dripping cord. Her ears roared. A new sound spluttered, distant, strange. It came to her that it was laughter, her own.

Now she waded deeper, letting the water take her weight, submerging, emerging, each dip timed with the motion of the waves. Old words washed back to her. *White horses.* Who had taught her that? Nurse? Her mother?

Dressing again was a trial. The cloth caught at her damp flesh, her fingers fumbled pins and ties. She combed her sand-heavy hair as best she could. Her sea-wrinkled hands refused gloves.

Seawater was already frilling her hem white as she stepped back up the beach. Her legs and arms rippled with the memory of the sea. Deep in the folds, tiny grains of sand pricked and polished her skin at each stride. She glowed so, she thought all must see the pink beaming through the mourning black. A soft breeze blew. Moistening her lips with her tongue, she tasted the intense, savoury tang of salt.

Gingerbread
Virginia Moffatt

Tea. for two. Two for tea... I am humming to myself as I mould the dough into four walls and two roof panels. Ginny has always loved my gingerbread houses – this will be the perfect welcome home.

The traffic is heavy as I leave Bristol. Stop... start... brake... clutch... I stutter along the road. At this rate I'll be lucky to reach Mum by four, and I have to be away by five. She'll be disappointed – but then she always is.

The gingerbread is too warm to shape. I'll put it in the fridge and have a cup of tea while I wait for it to cool and for Ginny to arrive. I'm looking forward to seeing her. She's a good girl, phones every Sunday as she has done since boarding school, but it's always so much better face to face.

At last I am on the forest road. The winter sun hangs low in the sky, perfectly placed to dazzle my eyes. The dashboard clock says three thirty; I should just make it. I told her not go to any bother but I expect she ignored me and is making a gingerbread house as usual.

It's been a while since Ginny visited. I realise children grow up and leave you, but I do miss the time when it was just the two of us. Back then, there was nothing I didn't know about her life. These days I'm not even sure how she's doing her hair, let alone who her friends are.

Before she sent me away, I used to love those gingerbread houses. I'd pretend to be Gretel, picking away at the walls, sucking the jelly dots and smarties, in the comforting knowledge no witch would ever do me any harm.

The fridge has done the trick so I begin to erect the house. This was always the part that Ginny enjoyed the most. She'd sit entranced by my ability to build walls and a roof from cake. Then she'd help me decorate, an eager slave, keen to do my bidding.

A herd of cows has blocked the road, stopping me in my tracks. Last time that happened we were on our way to the school I hated. I begged Mum to turn back but she refused - my education must come first. Which was when I realised witches were real. After that I lost the taste for gingerbread.

Something has gone wrong with the walls; I can't make them stay together. Ginny rings as the house collapses for the fourth time. She mumbles something about cows and having to turn back. Then she hangs up, driving off to her mysterious life in the city, a life that has no room for me.

I feel bad that I didn't make it, but those cows just wouldn't budge, and - as she taught me - work comes first.

I throw the broken cake in the bin. It'll be tea for one, as usual.

A Marionettist's Musings While on a Park Bench

Charley Karchin

Children never obey—not like exquisite marionettes that take long strides when I will them to. That walk or bend to touch their toes with no more than a flick of my wrist. Their eyes were always open and waiting for my next command. Children can be made to listen, but after a few hours their limbs become too stiff to be manipulated by the strings threaded through their palms and feet.

Bubblegum Barbie
Emily Devane

One day in August, Barbie moved in across the street. I was practising on my new roller skates.

I waved hello.

She blew a big pink bubble.

'That chest can't be real,' Gran whispered, ushering me inside. Mum was at work and Dad wasn't around to have an opinion.

Barbie was six feet tall and never wore the same outfit twice. My favourites were the dresses – occasionally so short that Gran winced. Barbie's hair changed colour every week, from blonde to auburn to slush puppy blue. She drove a convertible with cream leather seats. I liked to look at my face in its mirrors.

One day, when she'd been there a fortnight and her hair was vanilla with pink stripes, she crossed the street on rollerblades. A tiny dog trotted beside her.

'I call it *Ice-cream Sundae*,' she said.

'The poodle?' I asked.

'Ha, you're funny! I meant this crazy hair!' Her voice was milkshake thick. American, but different. 'Wanna skate with me?'

I nodded. She wore rollerblades. Her hotpants drew anxious glances from behind net curtains.

Whatever the whispers, she always made time to say hello, first stubbing out her cigarette with the pointed toe of her shoe, or the heel of her boot, or the edge of her sneaker.

'Hey pretty girl,' she'd say, curling a plastic nail beneath my chin.

One day, while I ate beans on toast for tea with Gran, we saw her getting into a stretch limo. 'Some people have all the fun,' Gran said.

'A-huh,' I said, in my best American accent.

According to my Mickey Mouse alarm clock, Barbie came home at 3am that night. A man kicked her door for a while, then left.

Next time I saw her, I asked about her car.

'It was never mine,' she said, 'it was just for borrow.'

'And the poodle?'

'That too.' She muttered something in a language I didn't understand. 'You okay, pretty girl?'

'Yes.' I said. The gum I was chewing had lost its flavour.

That night, there was shouting (at 4am Mickey Mouse time). And again the night after.

Barbie started jogging past me without speaking. I almost didn't recognise her. She wore a black tracksuit and a baseball cap pulled low over her face.

I drew her a picture: Barbie with ice-cream hair. *When I grow up*, I wrote, *I want to be like you*. I put it through her letterbox.

Then I sat on our front step, chewing gum. She crossed the street, crouched beside me, and took off her sunglasses.

'Wanna know something?'

'A-huh' I replied, blowing the tiniest of bubbles.

'Not bad,' she said. 'Trust me, sweetheart, you don't wanna be like me.' She blew the biggest bubble I'd ever seen, so big it touched my face.

I popped it with my finger.

'See you around,' she said, curling her finger beneath my chin one last time. 'Stay pretty. And funny. Stay funny, too.' Then she walked away with her headphones on, humming to herself.

Lifer

Adam Trodd

Tommy was a warrior. Got knocked down. Got up again. Assailed by life. We are strings of smoke he'd say. The slightest breeze. Light up. Start again. Tommy wore life as if it was a woollen jumper that scratched him to distraction. Cared too much. Strange to say but life got into his bones and made of him a haggard thing. Marked him. All this life all these people Tommy'd say and I'd understand what he meant but then again maybe not because I didn't let life seep into me like a toxin the way it did with Tommy. I get up go to work watch TV have dinner go to bed. Press. Repeat. A boulder that life swirled both sides of. Impassive. Immobile. We were both afraid of life for different reasons; Tommy because it was killing him. Me, I couldn't invite it in so I built walls and walls. We'd meet and I'd be in my office clothes. Anaesthetised. Watch checking. Wondering what I'm missing. Always looking for an out. And they'd come eventually, the questions.

'Do you ever think about it?'

'What, Tommy?'

'What he done?'

'What who done, Tommy?'

'To us...to you?'

'Finish your pint, Tommy.'

When he reached out for the glass I saw the marks. On his arm. Vampiric haematoma. The shock of it. I wanted to hug him. Wanted to cry. Couldn't.

When people ask me what my brother died of I just say life.

Shirts – A Fable
R.J. Dent

Iulia Hasdeu made shirts.

They were the most beautiful shirts in the world. Hardly anyone knew though, because Iulia only made them for immediate family, and on very special occasions.

One such occasion was the graduation of her grandson, Octavian Goga; awarded an honours degree in Environmental Economics from Sapienta University.

Pride blazing in her eyes, she handed him the multi-coloured, beautifully embroidered linen shirt. He accepted the gift humbly, kissing his grandmother's cheek.

"Thank you, Grandmother," he said.

Back in Bucharest, Octavian showed his gift to his friends. They were impressed with the shirt's quality and beauty. Marcea Dinescu, a textiles graduate, wanted to meet Iulia. She explained her reasons, and requested Octavian's support.

Octavian readily agreed and arranged the meeting. Over tea and muffins, Marcea persuaded Iulia to produce more of her exquisite shirts – and make her family very rich.

Conscientious custodian of her family's welfare, Iulia agreed, insisting on a significant percentage of the gross, and the power to revoke the agreement if she became dissatisfied with any aspect of the shirt making.

Within hours, sewing and embroidery machines and hot presses were installed in a back room of Iulia's home. Textiles students were shipped in and set to work, diligently following Iulia's instructions.

Within three days, ten shirts had been made and quality approved by Iulia. They were wrapped and shipped to a Bucharest outlet, which sold all ten shirts within two days. The retailer telephoned for more. Marcea agreed to send more once the money for the previous shirts was deposited into her account. One day later, she received the money. After she had paid Iulia her agreed percentage, Marcea sent the retailer ten more of the beautiful shirts. Again they sold quickly. This time the money was prompt, so Marcea sent ten more shirts.

As the weeks passed, it became obvious that Marcea needed to send more than ten shirts every five days. She got in more machines, more textiles students and increased production to twenty shirts a week.

They all sold.

Marcea ordered more linen and more embroidery thread.

When the students restarted their work, they noticed that the quality of the linen was not as good as the cloth they had been using previously. They informed Marcea, who examined the linen, agreed and telephoned the supplier.

He told her that she'd had the best rolls of linen months ago, and that the ones she had just been sent, although made with poorer quality flax, were the only ones available.

Marcea accepted a discount.

Iulia examined a finished shirt and shook her head.

"No."

And she refused to quality approve them.

Marcea argued – to no avail.

Iulia made everyone leave. Her family heaved the machines out onto the street.

Marcea, having tasted success, took the machines, the raw materials and the workforce back to Bucharest. She set them up in a rented house and made one hundred shirts in five days.

So far, not one of those shirts has been sold.

Sam, 29
Martha Gleeson

You need to run, now. I can't just run, I need to wait for the police. *You've done your bit, you called them, now get going.* They said to wait. *Sure, and when they get here they'll arrest you and it's over.* They won't arrest—*Of course they will. Ex-con stood next to a dead body in an alleyway, they're going to arrest you.* But...I called it in. I didn't do it. *They won't see it that way.* I was never violent, they know that, it was just theft. *Do you really think they'll care? They'll see your rap sheet and that's it, you're done for.* But I didn't do it... *Since when do the cops care about fact? Now get going, there's no-one around and they won't be long.* I...I don't know what to do. I can't just leave him here. *Yes you can, you move one foot and then the other, preferably quickly. Go.* But... *Go. Now. Move.* Oh God... *Just don't look back.*

Three Kids, Two Balloons
K.M. Elkes

We are late, again, because The Eldest tore a wing off The Youngest's dress and The Middle One refused her shoes. There's a nip to the air and a cellar-black sky and as I magnificently outlined on the journey down, this 'communidy fete' is a dismal, nearly-over, affair.

The face painters have knocked off early and the only thing that lingers in the food tent is a stink of onions and the buttery tang of trodden grass. The children are salty-faced for entertainment, but the stage only holds a thin girl wailing poetry with the voice of a cracked oboe.

Then we see the Balloon Man, a rump of a fella trailing two last globes, the runts of the litter, the last chance salooners, saggy as bingo wings.

"We'll take them," my wife declares and gives up twice the money she ought. Transferred to other hands, the two balloons sink further on their strings, like geriatric dogs lying down in hot gutters.

"Now then," she says and hands them to me. The children look up like tiny open beaked birds, expectant of an equal share.

"Now then what? "I say. "How does this work?"

"Just…keep a hold of them for now."

I wish for a brief moment we had arrived early, so I could throw cash at Balloon Man for his whole stock, until I could drift up, hearing faint voices: "My daddy can fly. My daddy is a spaceman. See him soar." But I know I would look down at my wife's disapproving face, see her pull up a sock or wipe a face, knowing I'd let go soon because I don't have the strength to cling on.

At home, the three children eye each other, then the balloons. There are knives in those looks, howitzers, the shelling of their respective positions will be thunderous and sustained.

"Here's the thing," I say. "These two poor balloons are missing the third one. Just like you Katie and Anna would miss Jack, or Jack and Katie would miss Anna. Or any other combination thereof."

I'm flagging already, but they sit, prepared to go with this for a while. I look to my wife.

She takes things on apace. She busies them writing out a little card, a plea for a missing balloon. They are liberal with glitter and glue, then add some extra, then brighten the table, floor and cat.

We go out into the garden tying the balloons together then tethering the sparkling card. There is a degree of solemnity in the dusk air. The five of us gather in and let the balloons go and the five of us stand to watch them rise, wobbling, directionless and odds on certain to rupture on a rooftop or flail into some half-distant wires.

But for a few vital seconds they do their damnedest to soar and somehow that seems enough.

Who? What?

Ashley Chantler

Tony switches on the kettle, gets the semi-skimmed from the fridge, wishes he had some booze. Felicity and he have just got back from a talk at their local library. It was titled 'Writing on the [Woman's] Body: /De/Familiarizing the "Other"' and delivered by an obese lady with a smile he couldn't read. He'd reminded Felicity that it was quiz night at the Jolly Duck, but she'd reminded him that he's an idiot.

'Tea or coffee?' he shouts towards the lounge.

'Tea. Two sugars.'

He didn't understand everything the lady had said, but the gist seemed to be that contemporary women authors are voicing the previously silent or unseen. The handout's first quotation was from Sujata Bhatt's 'White Asparagus':

Who speaks of the strong currents
streaming through the legs, the breasts
of a pregnant woman
in her fourth month?

Tony doesn't know, but feels he's done something wrong. He frowns and pours the milk.

Taking the mugs of tea to the lounge, he stands in the doorway, spreads his arms, coughs.

Felicity looks up. 'What the hell are you doing?'

Tony is naked from the waist down, except for a pair of grey socks. 'Who speaks of *my* strong currents? Who speaks for the individual that is *me*?' He was going to add 'And why the fuck should they?' but didn't get the chance.

'You really are an idiot. Give me my tea and put those things away.'

Pub Quiz
Alison Wassell

They make a great team. Andy does politics and current affairs, Tom does sport and geography, Stella does history, and what the men refer to as 'all the arty-farty stuff.' Andy's girlfriend does anything to do with celebrities, fashion, and all that crap. The girlfriend changes, from week to week, but the type never does.

Stella loves the way Tom shields their answers from the team on the next table with his body, like a little schoolboy. It makes her want to ruffle his hair. She nudges his foot under the table. His face crinkles into a smile.

Andy's girlfriend of the week is called Lucy. She is even blonder than usual. She giggles a lot. Stella smiles indulgently, seeing no real harm in her. Her top leaves little to the imagination. She's not Tom's type, though. Stella watches him carefully. His eyes don't stray to Lucy's cleavage at all. He concentrates on his blunt pencil, and their answers. Stella puts her hand on his shoulder. He winks at her.

There is a round on current cabinet ministers. A photocopied sheet is distributed. Andy recognises them all. Lucy says she doesn't even know who the Prime Minister is. Is it still Tony Blair? They all laugh, pretending she's joking. She comes into her element in the next round, which is about the ridiculous names celebrities give to their babies. Tom smiles at her, and she simpers. Stella glares at the pair of them. Tom returns to his pencil.

There are some questions about FA Cup Finals, and goal scorers. Tom doesn't do that well. He seems preoccupied.

There is a round on paintings. Everyone else groans. Stella smiles, waiting for her chance to shine.

'Which Pre-Raphaelite artist painted a famous image of Ophelia in 1852?' says the landlord. There are more groans. Stella gives a smug little smirk.

'Rossetti,' she says. Tom asks her to spell it. She tells him how many 's's and how many 't's. He writes it down.

'It was Millais,' says Lucy. She sounds very sure. Tom crosses out his answer and writes the new one. Stella glares at him. He looks down at the table.

They win. They are the only team that knew Millais. They split the prize money between them and say a cheerful goodbye in the car park. Tom pecks Lucy on the cheek. He calls her Lucky Lucy. As he opens the car door Stella lays her hand on his arm. She grinds her heel into his foot. He winces. There is fear in his eyes. Stella's fingers press into his flesh. She told him what would happen, if he ever humiliated her again.

Sushi and Kitty Cats
Kaitlyn Johnson

What was it that made you stop and take notice? Was it my smile? Was it just big enough to be inviting but small enough to avoid appearing manic? Do you even remember what made you exchange those first few messages with me? Did you move past my picture and read what I claimed my personality was? Did you care to know that much? What words triggered your interest? Could you have connected with the Firefly references, the Buffy fangirling? Did you think I'd recognize my own words, each of my likes and dislikes parroted back to me in your first invitation to chat? Was that supposed to set you apart from the rest? So, you got to know me for more than my picture, right? That meant I should take a chance on you?

Can you believe how careless I was? How I let a complete stranger drive me around to what we now call our first date? Have you thought back on that night? Does it still sound like a good time to you? A good start? Were you really excited for your first sushi experience, an event you'd endure all because my profile said it was a favourite? Did you see the rice and fish and soy sauce and think, "What the hell am I doing here?" Did I talk about my cat too much? Were the patches of fur I'd missed with the lint roller noticeable?

It could've ended right there and then, am I right? Would you have given up if I'd said no to another night out, or would you have been interested enough to try winning me over? What would've happened had we not driven to your place, if we'd said goodnight and gone separate ways? How would life be different? Were you nervous when you asked me up to your apartment? Did you turn on the TV just so I'd be distracted? So I'd miss the subtle glances toward the bedroom? Are you sure you weren't just a little eager? Could you see I was? Our second date, what if it was too soon? Did I make the right sounds? Did I look beautiful?

Has there ever been a moment you regretted meeting me? For the cat toys littered all over the floor, the scratches like stretch marks on your couch? You say it happens, comes with the territory, but are you secretly fuming inside? Does the fact you swear every time she darts beneath your feet at night mean you're really upset? Is she a burden, or am I the one who trips you up? Does your constant acceptance of every little flaw mean you're in love?

It is love, isn't it? Big love? Is it okay to believe that?

Desert Blossom
Annie Evett

Andy clutched his bunch of blossoms as he steadied himself on the crowded bus. A waft of stale sweat, thickened with fine desert dust swirled around him uncomfortably. Looking at the wilting floral arrangement optimistically, he picked out bent leaves and tried to straighten them within the dusty cellophane. "Callie won't mind. She knows it's the best I can do." Andy blinked quickly; tears drying instantly in the heat. "I promised to come back."

Scorching wind hit him like a fan-forced oven as he stepped off the bus. Groups of workers squatted along the roads and eyed him with suspicion. Soldiers stood with huge rifles propped casually on their khaki clad hips. One smiled through grey teeth, greeting Andy in a mishmash of languages. "Where you going?" Swinging his gun onto his back, he gestured to Andy "Want a guide? Very special price, my friend."

Andy readjusted his backpack. "Shukran." Shaking his head, "Mish ayiza." His Arabic failed him as he weakly pointed up the road. "Valley of the Queens."

The solider waved. "Ma'assalama."

Sand blew into Andy's eyes. "He wasn't a year ago." He held his breath as tears threatened. He scanned the valley, not surprised to see industrious pockets of workmen throughout, but few tourists.

Silhouetted along the skyline, Andy spotted outposts of soldiers with machine guns. As he walked towards the ruins, calls of greetings and offers to guide or assist him, grew. Andy thanked them through gritted teeth and continued till he reached the sandstone stairs.

He breath became ragged as he carefully counted the stairs, stopping at the twenty fourth.

Reverently, Andy laid down the wilting blossoms, and

touching the edge of the stair, noted it had not been replaced. His fingers traced the perfect bullet hole and found the place Callie had last breathed.

Premiums
Ian Shine

When my girlfriend lost her job I got sick of her asking for money, so I paid to make her mobile into a premium-rate number. Paying £1.49 a minute to hear the things she said about hosing down the car and marinating meat drove me crazy. Even when I got home I couldn't stop calling, and would sneak into the bathroom to dial her number.

My phone charges eventually got so high I had to get a second job at nights to be able to pay our rent and bills, but this gave me far less time to spend listening to her talk, as mobiles were banned on the factory floor. Whenever I did find time to chat, she'd spend most of the call moaning about how her income had started to decline and she was forced to go around the house wearing nothing but dirty, threadbare clothes that barely covered her up at all.

So I started ringing her from the office phone at my day job, but the boss soon found out and I got fired. The money from my second job wasn't enough to cover our living costs and the price of keeping her premium-rate line open, so I had to shut her down and tell her to go back to work.

Now when I call her standard mobile she doesn't pick up, and every time I ask her to talk at home she shakes a tin can in front of me. I can't afford to pay, so I just have to watch her clean the car and make dinner, wearing rags that don't leave much to the imagination. It's nowhere near as much fun.

Misunderstanding
Vivien Jones

Geraldine gets off a train at the wrong station. Dozing in the overheated train, she mishears the mangled public address announcement saying 'Cumnock' for 'Kilmarnock'; in a panic she gathers bags and coat and gets off the train. The sprinter races off before she realises. It's an un-manned station so she finds a phone box and phones home. Down the line comes a humiliating telephone tirade from her husband. He tells her how useless she is and instructs her to find a B&B for the night. He'll phone her sister in Kilmarnock and explain. It takes her three times walking the main street before she has to accept that the only accommodation offered is in the pub. The landlady is reluctant on a single night B&B shout in the middle of winter but she ups the rate by 50%, then leads the way to an unheated room upstairs. Geraldine asks about a meal and the landlady says there's a chip shop at the end of the street. She could have a drink at the bar and any of five flavours of crisps. Geraldine asks for coffee and the landlady grimaces - *it'll just be instant* - so they go back down to the bar.

She's sitting alone sipping hot coffee when she's aware of a man over close to her. He smiles, tells her his name is Mike and, with a wink, asks her where she's been all his life. She laughs, not at his absurdity but suddenly aware that no-one at this precise moment knows where she is, who she is or where she's been. Something wild rushes through her, the idea of twelve hours of anonymity. When Mike offers to show her the chippie she says yes. Then she says yes to a walk through the play park and sits on a swing laughing at his foolish talk. Mike thinks he's doing well so far and so does she. Their walk back to the pub is slow, their talk soft, their eyes roving each other's person under the lamplight. At the bar, the landlady bets the barman a fiver on the outcome of the evening, then she serves Mike a double whisky and Geraldine a large sweet sherry.

Geraldine pays for both and several more.

The room upstairs at last finds use. Mike is a thoughtful lover and Geraldine has a long-held grudge to expunge. Supping vengeance she throws herself into their romp with a novel abandon. She reaches a noisy orgasm for the first time since her honeymoon, fleetingly remembering her husband's disgust at her cries. Mike is happy to reap the rewards of whatever is fuelling her energies. After a couple of hours she wishes him goodnight and shuts the door behind him. He is bemused. She sleeps like a baby.

Next morning she is on Cumnock Station platform waiting for the 8.03am Sprinter to Kilmarnock, thinking *well there's Edinburgh and Jedburgh, Inverkeithing and Innerleithen.* There's a little smile on her face.

Wakes Week
David Hartley

Sis can't talk much because of her phossy jaw. She got her phossy jaw from the matches she makes in her factory. It makes a hole in her face, I don't like looking at it. She don't like talking now, because of her phossy jaw. It's Wakes Week in Bury. We have the week off to do other things. I don't know what to do. Sis tries to sell matches in the streets so I help her. She don't sell many. I asked her why it's called Wakes Week. She held a hand to her jaw and said; *it's when the world wakes up.*

I didn't understand. She said she'd show me. She stands one end of the street and I stay at the other. She waves and I can still see her and I wave too. The air has gone away. We can see all the way along the streets now. Then she takes me to the roof of the factory. It's dangerous and not allowed but I trust sis and she smiles to show me it's okay. I can see a long, long way. It is the most beautiful thing I've ever seen, apart from when Sis didn't have her phossy jaw.

We count the chimneys. There are lots and lots, more than ten. I only thought there was two: mine and Sis's. But there are lots and lots, more than ten. She sits me on her knee and holds up my hand and we point at the chimneys and she tells me where they are. *That one's Preston, that one's Blackpool, that one's Burnley, that one's Accrington, that one's Bolton, that one's Wigan, that one's Stalybridge.* I know it hurts Sis to say these words, but it is brilliant to see the whole world wake up. It is all factories like ours, and I think that is amazing. I wonder if there is anyone in the world who could fix Sis's phossy jaw, so I ask her, but she shakes her head and frowns. I know what that means. It means; *stop asking questions now.*

So I stop asking questions. Instead, I count the chimneys again. There are lots and lots, more than ten.

Burning Faith
Frankie McMillan

After the tourists leave and nobody wants to pay to see a fire breather on the street, I go back to working in the half-way house. What the residents are half way to isn't clear but today is Creative Therapy day and I've run out of glue for the paper mache so I tell them we'll be fire-eaters instead. We'll start by putting a lighted match in our mouths. They'll need to open up wide, otherwise they'll burn. It's science, I tell them. Once they close their mouths the flame will go out.

The residents all sit around the big table so I can keep an eye on them. And when one of the guys asks me how long it would take to die if they swallowed a lighted match I say don't even think about it. This exercise is a confidence booster, I say. After swallowing fire, you can do anything. That's when the new resident walks in.

Faith. She could be anybody's grandmother; wears thick pantyhose the colour of mouse skin. She holds her head erect and speaks in complete sentences but her hands and feet constantly twitch under the table. Faith wants to please; whatever therapy, whatever programme, whatever pill is on offer, she will co-operate. So when it's her turn to put the lighted match in her mouth, she obediently opens her puckered lips. For a second her hand shakes. She winces, tries to close her mouth over the burning match. 'Right over, sweetheart,' I urge. 'Right over, until the flame's out.' Someone else tugs my arm. They want to go onto the next step, winding cotton wool around the fire wands and I get distracted.

Later I see Faith at the sink swallowing water. The front of her gingham blouse is wet. 'Are you okay?' I ask and she nods. But I know she's not okay, she's probably got a blister on her tongue and she's probably blaming herself, *stupid Faith* but I don't say anything. 'Thank you,' she whispers. And when six months later Faith runs out onto the road in her nightie, flings herself in front of a cartage truck, everyone sits in a circle and says what they remember about her. One girl, still in her pink pyjamas and Ugg boots, tells of her surprise when Faith first walked into the house. She'd been her Bible teacher in Year Nine and she thought if Miss Ewing was here with a mental illness then anybody could get a mental illness. And she felt less of a freak for that.

Then the staff tell their stories but when they turn to me I don't say anything about the day we put matches in our mouths. I close my eyes, remembering in my own way. Faith. She holds the lighted match to her lips, thrusts it inside and for a glorious second the roof of her mouth lights up like a cathedral.

Pigeon English
David Cook

Dom walked past the pigeon, which said 'Alright, mate?'

He stopped, and looked at the bird. 'Did you just say something?' he asked.

'Course not, mate, I'm a bloody pigeon,' said the pigeon.

'Bugger me, a talking pigeon,' exclaimed Dom.

'Read my beak,' said the pigeon. 'I am not a talking pigeon. Coo, bloody coo, OK?'

'No, no, you're speaking now,' said Dom. 'I heard it.'

'Nah, mate. You're cracking up, that's what it is. Voices in the head and that, innit. I'd see a doctor, if I were you.'

'What? No, you're bloody well talking!'

'Am not! You ask that lot.'

Dom turned to the crowd at the bus station, who all managed to look away simultaneously while being sure to keep watching, which is quite a skill when you think about it.

'You heard it, right?' he demanded. 'That pigeon spoke!'

The crowd avoided eye contact. A few people shook their heads.

'See mate,' said the pigeon. 'You've gone round the twist. Loco in the coconut. Nuts in the nut. Check yerself into a clinic, that's my advice.'

Dom looked around desperately. The crowd were all taking a tremendous interest in the timetable for the number 42.

Then a small voice piped up. 'I heard him talking, mister!' it said.

Dom wheeled round in joy. He wasn't going mad after all.

'A talking pigeon, who'd ever of thought it?' said the rat by his foot.

Kittiwakes
Catherine Edmunds

Death doesn't have time to waste at this time of year. He comes quickly and sits down beside Margery Ellison. She's relieved to see him at last and to find he's short and a bit overweight. He looks like that actor who was in that thing. She tells him, and he's delighted. They chat for a while about this and that, then he tells her it's time to go. She's not sure how this works, but he says, not to worry, just think about sky and sea, white cottages and kittiwakes.

But Margery doesn't like kittiwakes. She's lived in Newcastle all her life and has been bombed under the Tyne Bridge on more than one occasion. She stares Death in the eye.

No, she says. I don't think that's going to work.

Death is confused. The kittiwakes have never failed before.

Music? he says. How about Auld Lang Syne?

Can't bear it, says Margery.

Not even sung by choirs of angels?

Margery turns her head away. She'd had such high hopes of Death. A tear trickles from her eye onto the pillow. She can hear the nurses going about their business beyond the curtains they've drawn round the bed. She would rather like a cup of tea. She tells Death as much. He's about to answer when there's a call for him from the other end of the ward – it's urgent, a sudden cardiac arrest. Margery will have to wait.

Once he's gone, Margery takes stock. She finds she doesn't want to die just yet. First of all she wants to shoot a kittiwake with her father's old gun, his thunder bus as she used to call it. It was huge and heavy and pitted with age, but it wouldn't half make a mess of those blasted birds. Might damage the bridge, which would be a shame, but worth it just to see the feathers flying and the squawking – and the sharp-suited man from the hotel cheering because he's always going on at the council to get rid of the birds so that they don't shit on his customers.

Kittiwake shit is the worst. Margery had a budgie once, and it made tiny little pellets of poo, almost dry, but kittiwakes!

She lies back and smiles, remembering Bobby, the feel of his toes curling round her finger, his little head bobbing up and down as he went through his repertoire of clever Bobby, and who's a pretty boy then?

The commotion at the other end of the ward has settled. Death is back. He asks how she's feeling. A bit better now, she says. I've been thinking about Bobby.

Would you like to see him again, asks Death.

Oh yes. Yes.

Death takes her by the hand and leads her away. She has a feeling she's been tricked. She wasn't ready.

What a clever boy.

The Door Closes
Kevlin Henney

GEORGIE: Pretty!
JAMIE: Huh, pretty weird.
JESSIE: Pretty gross.
ALEX: I wonder how they got like that? Why they're here?

Alex kneels down to look, the other three follow. Four birds, stacked atop one another on the forest floor in the centre of a clearing. Late afternoon sun is disappearing behind clouds, shifting the colours of the birds and leaves around them into darker shades. The four lean in.

JAMIE: I dare you.
JESSIE: Touch one? No way!
GEORGIE: Shh. Sleeping.
JESSIE: Sleeping? No, Georgie, dead!

Georgie's face falls. Alex picks up a twig and pokes the smallest bird, the apex of the pyramid, then the largest one at the base, gently so as not to topple the arrangement.

ALEX: Yes, definitely dead. But definitely like this on purpose.
JAMIE: Maybe it's art? Like on that autumn trail we came here for last year.
JESSIE: But it's still winter.
ALEX: Jessie's right. Wrong time of year. Besides, the art trail was signposted and near the paths. This is something else.
JESSIE: Someone put them here after they were dead.
JAMIE: But how did they die? Did the someone find them then put them like this?
JESSIE: Or did the someone kill them?

Alex leans closer, sees flecks of blood on the lighter-coloured birds.

ALEX: I don't know. But I think we should get back. Mum and Dad will be wondering where we are.
JESSIE: I thought we were lost?
ALEX: We are. Looking at these birds isn't going to help us get

unlost. It'll be evening soon and Mum and Dad will be worried.

JAMIE: She's not your Mum.

GEORGIE: Not your Dad!

Jamie scowls at Georgie.

ALEX: Whatever. Mum — or Sam — and Dad — or Chris — will be worried. We've been gone too long.

JESSIE: I said we shouldn't have left the path.

JAMIE: Liar! You chased that squirrel and we followed you.

JESSIE: But I said we should go back.

JAMIE: Only after Georgie poked you in the eye with a stick and you started crying.

JESSIE: I didn't cry!

ALEX: Quiet. Georgie... where's Georgie? Georgie!

Georgie peeks out from behind a tree at the edge of the clearing.

GEORGIE: Look! More.

The three run over. A faint trail leads out of the clearing. Four squirrels are stacked against one of the trees, as still and silent and flecked as the four birds. Further on the trail becomes more clearly defined. The four can see some kind of coloured cairn. Cairn? Foxes, stacked — four?

GEORGIE: Look, house!

JESSIE: Perhaps whoever lives there knows the forest and can help us find our way back.

They can just make out a shack at the end of the path. Wooden and weather-beaten, its door is reddened and ajar. Georgie starts off down the path.

ALEX: No. No, I don't think they can. Not that way, Georgie. Let's go the other way.

The four return to the clearing and keep walking.

The door closes.

Clippers

Debbi Voisey

'I can't find them.'

'Look harder, dig deeper, they're there.' Her voice muffled around a mouthful of apple.

Her hair looked perfect. Long and flowing like ears of corn in a windswept field. I loved it. She did too, but this was important to her.

In the drawer I shoved aside the letter, in the white envelope with the jagged edges from where we had ripped it open frantically; fearfully. The stamp - "University Hospital" – was partially visible.

And then there they were; the clippers.

'Are you sure about this?' I watched her throw the apple core into the bin; flick her hair.

She could not take her eyes off the clippers in my hand – I felt that I could hypnotise her by moving them back and forth.

'Do it,' she said, a barely audible tremor in her voice. 'I want to be with you every step of the way.'

I Go on the Morrow to Murder the King

Joy Myerscough

I go with the day's break to London. I go to murder the King. Aye, and his parliament, too. I go to avenge your death, Mistress Clitherow.

The gunpowder is purchased. The plans are laid. Kit and his men wait at Westminster for me. We must prevail, for God is on our side, and the year of our Lord 1605 will be remembered as the year our country turned back to the one true faith.

Tonight I sup at the Star and Anchor; a tankard of ale sits before me, and a supper of cabbage and beef. My rosary comforts me, though I darest not take it out.

Mary, Mother of God, bless my endeavors.

Men sit around me, talking of desultory matters: the flooding of the river's banks, the lack of fresh meats in the Shambles, the petty thief hanged today on the Knavesmire; even now his corpse swings from the noose.

Mistress Clitherow: that day on the bridge lives on in my heart. They stripped you, laid you face down, a sharp rock between your shoulder blades, a wooden plank on top, and four men hauled from the gutter to effect your demise. You know not how many nights I have lain sleepless, wishing I'd had the courage to put my rosary in your hand that day. I was but sixteen: a pitiful excuse. Would that I meet my own end with your courage and faith.

And what crime had you committed? Only that of practising the True Faith. Only that of being a friend to the persecuted. Only that of aiding our priests.

I vow you did not die in vain, Mistress.

God have mercy on us both. I go on the morrow to murder the King.

Special Delivery
Calum Kerr

It was a Tuesday, so Dave was thinking about killing himself, as he did every day.

He was not expecting the doorbell to ring, nor a parcel to be delivered.

He sat and examined the box, but the label gave nothing away: a printed address with no return information.

Inside were five smaller packages, wrapped in chip-shop-plain paper, each with a number written on it. He unwrapped the first package.

It contained a smaller box holding a doll. No, not a doll a ... what did you call them? ... an action figure.

But this wasn't a superhero or whatever. It was a doll of him. A doll of Dave; Dave from ago.

It was wearing the stone-wash denim jeans, the white socks and slip-on shoes, the cream cardigan over a white t-shirt, which had been his teenage uniform. It even had the same floppy hair.

Dave ran his hand over the millimetres-long, salt-and-pepper fuzz which now covered his head, and sighed.

He stared at it, trying to understand, then finally put it down and reached for the next package.

It was the same, except different. This was an older Dave, with the black leather pants and fitted leather jacket of his early twenties. It even came with a small crash helmet with a miniature rendition of the scratch it received when that Fiesta knocked him off near the big Tesco's.

Third was him in suit and tie. His wedding suit.

He didn't look at that one for long.

The fourth had the black suit he wore to the funeral. He put that doll aside without a second glance.

The final doll was him today. It had the baggy jogging pants, the stained sweatshirt, the stubble, the reddened eyes, and came packaged with its own bottle of tablets.

He stared at that one for a long, long time before he put it down with the others.

As afternoon wore on towards evening he sat and remembered all the lives he'd lived.

And then the doorbell rang again.

It was the same driver. He'd forgotten the '2 of 2'.

This box only held one, larger package, marked '6'.

He unwrapped it with shaking hands.

It contained another doll, another effigy of him, but this one was wearing an outfit that Dave had never owned. He didn't have a t-shirt like that, nor a pair of trousers in that shade of blue.

And the accompanying woman was a stranger to him. From what he could see of her plastic features, she was very pretty.

The way her slim figure was interrupted by a bulging belly seemed even more attractive.

The accessories included a pram and the tiniest of dummies.

Dave held it in his hands and stared at it as the tears ran down his cheeks and the day eased its way into evening.

Even in the dark, he didn't relinquish the box. He sat there and waited, knowing that eventually it would get light again.

Grains

Joanna Campbell

The leaves of the table are folded down these days. The cloth reaches the floor. The house, its ceilings now too high, has settled into a silence so deep we can hear the pump humming in the fish tank. Reminders remain; two dull fish, a stack of old school French books, fingerprints on the living-room wall.

It takes so little time to wash up two plates, one small knife and fork, one slender pair of chopsticks.

When I found you, it seemed you were living in the silt of a pool, almost drowned, looking up at dark shapes swimming beneath the sunlit surface. When I beckoned, you saw my shadow and emerged, gasping.

The others are so much older than you, adults before I was ready. And they have left, one by one, discovering important travels, other homes. They never learned to nurture a project. They excel at leaving things behind.

Today we made a picture frame. I urged you to follow the patterns in the wood, aligning them to avoid stress and distortion. You looked at me, your black eyes solemn, and began again. You dovetailed the joints, yet did not match the direction of the grain.

I ask you to make a beautiful picture for the frame, something to capture your spirit, expecting pagodas and plum blossoms. And I hope for water, a tribute to my allegorical pool.

"Let her be herself," the others said before they went, tired of China in the house.

I am not allowed to see your work. You want it in place first. You send me out of the room, telling me to wait in the hall. In the cold draught that flaps through the letterbox, I stand on the other side of the door and listen to your gentle tapping, your shallow breath gathering speed.

When I am called in to see it, I try not to mind. I force a smile and smooth my hand over the silk curve of your hair.

You did not understand what I meant about making a beautiful picture of your home.

You have not made a picture at all.

At dinner, I persevere with the chopsticks while you eat your fish-fingers and beans with the knife and fork. We fall out of our table rhythm today. You are going to win.

I am still chasing the final few grains of rice in my bowl as you put your cutlery together, slightly askew, and ask to get down.

"Yes," I say. "I'm lagging a little behind you."

I look again at the frame. It hangs crooked. Within it, the others' grimy handprints, stamped on the wall long ago, lie off-centre.

Panda
Fat Roland

The sign, written by one of the humans, said some human words. The panda squinted at the sign across the walkway for two hours or two days, piecing together the letters until she understood.

Chicken shed closed.

The sign said *Chicken shed closed.* The panda did some thinking. She thought of the chicken enclosure being closed and the zoo being without chickens.

She walked around a leaf-strewn stretch of grass until she found a large strip of bark she had clawed from a tree some minutes or hours ago. She scratched into the bark. She made some symbols. The panda read back the symbols.

Zoo cannot be without chickens, what to do?

She checked the symbols for spelling. An ant scuttled along the front of the tyre swing and stopped to watch the panda. The panda saw the ant. The panda flattened the ant with her paw. This was a good system, and she thought about how good this system was. Within minutes or hours, a colony of ants gathered around the body.

The panda nudged the strip of scratched bark towards them and the ants set to work. They scuttled under the bark and carried out the panda's message on their backs. They left her enclosure under loose fencing. They would be in the lion field before dawn or by next week or by any time at all.

The lions would know what to do. That's why they were in charge. She pictured the lions as 20 metres tall with two dozen arms and teeth instead of fur. The panda thought about what she had done, about the symbols in the bark and how clever she was. The sign had said *Chicken shed closed.* A zoo cannot be without chickens.

She felt a feeling inside her stomach. She saw some bamboo on a log. She sniffed the bamboo then grimaced at the bamboo. The panda did this a lot until the shadows grew longer.

Sometimes the ants didn't come back. She wondered if the ants ever came back.

The panda looked at the darkening sky and then at the shadows. She squinted again at the sign across the walkway. This time the human letters on the human sign, now lit by fluorescent lights, formed more quickly. She understood better now.

Chip shop closed.

The sign said *Chip shop closed.*

The panda patted the tyre swing but it barely moved. The rope was brown and frayed. She tried to think of a time when there were chickens in the zoo, if ever there were chickens in the zoo. She played with this thought for two hours or two days. The stars made arcs across the sky.

Fish Supper
Laura Tickle

Mother cries as she tries to get the insides out of the fish. Not because she feels sad for the thing but because she can't 'gut the bastard'. As she tries to shear through its tail, she pushes down on its belly so hard that its stomach explodes out of its mouth and its eyes shoot across the room like little mushy cannonballs.

Mother turns around. She is shaking and her face is rigid. I notice the little soft glob that's caught in her eyelashes and realise what's wrong. The eye of the fish is sitting on the bow of mascara that lines her own eye and I'm suddenly aware of her white knuckles and the knife in her hand. She is puffing hot breath in and out of her nose and mouth and her face is getting redder and redder. I point across the room to where Trevor is lying, making a steamy, dog-shaped print on the floor. The other fish eye has landed in the thick, curly hair on his back. I smile hoping she will join in but she screams and stabs at the fish like it's a spider she wants to squash.

'Fucking, shitting, blunt, fucking, butter knife.'

Her kitten heels don't stand a chance when they hit the puddle of blood and she skids across the room, fish and knife still in hand. She squeals, Russian squat dancing as she tries to keep herself standing. She hits the floor with a crack and lies on her back, crying, with her dress up around her waist. I can see her stockings.

Dad opens the kitchen door and there are scales and guts and bones on the cupboards and on the ceiling and in my hair. There is an intestine on the floor that looks like a deflated balloon and me and dad and the dog look at it, then at each other, but none of us say a word.

The Vineyard
Catherine McNamara

They were advised to remove the vineyard. The grape trunks had heavy unruly kinks and were clothed in moss, and the vines that sprang along the wires were each summer weaker and less adorned with fruit. A fast-growing more modern plant was suggested, a hybrid that would show results within three years. It was a soft, easy decision to make given their father had passed last year, so there was no wrath in the room or fists on the table, just the three brothers (Valerio after the car smash had remained slow and staring), one of whom was in the military and mostly concerned with his rebellious daughter, the other was dully married, and the youngest, Maurizio, who as a boy had told blazing lies but now ably managed the property with his wife Sonia, who was accepting and stifled.

The wires that ran through the grape plants were cut and coiled for further usage. The concrete posts that rose every three paces were hoisted out of the earth: this occurred on a day that Maurizio hired three additional Romanian labourers. When all that remained standing were the rows of limbless grape trunks, Maurizio used his power saw to cut each down, as close as possible to the dirt. The following week he would bring out the digger to overturn the root systems. Then this long job would be half done. The wood gave off a stricken oily odour as he went along.

Maurizio's wife Sonia watched his progress from an upper vineyard where she was pruning. These *tocai* plants they always left to the end as they were drier and less prone to sickness, and also the most attractive part of the property to work. She stood along an arcade of cropped vines and stopped the compressor for a moment, watching her husband at work. The severed grape trunks had fallen messily in his wake, where Sonia would have told him to stack them to one side. Half the vineyard now lay felled every which way on the wet winter grass. Sonia saw how Maurizio half-knelt with the chainsaw in his lap, and she listened to the whining sound that rose and fell as he sliced through each one then moved on to the next. She thought of the stash of new green plants in their plastic pockets of fertilised soil, waiting in the barn, how they emanated an unreal eagerness. For a moment she imagined her husband's heartbreak should these young plants fall lifeless to the ground; how he would sit at the table and she would protect him from his critical brothers.

Behind Sonia the sloping vineyard met a stone support wall that harboured snake litters in the summer, and above this a gravel road encircled the rocky hill but led nowhere. Neighbours of hers dumped rubbish there; youngsters buzzed around on motorcross bikes, boys stoned cats, and puppies were abandoned.

The Pleasure Principle
Rob Walton

Don emptied The Brown Cow's outdoor ashtray into his Lidl Bag 4 Life.

He then returned to the flat, knocked the lager cans off the living room coffee table, and disassembled.

He scratched and groaned. A piss-poor collection. At this time of the year only the diehard braved the elements to sit in the special areas or beer gardens. Quality smokers of quality cigarettes weren't tempted, even by space heaters. He had a quantity/quality paradox. Monied smokers would leave longer butts of better quality cigarettes, but they were few and far between. Those butts were in terracotta plant pots on professionally-installed decking. The tab ends he had before him were short and cheap. He would have to reduce his prices, and he had presents to buy.

His product wasn't the most desirable but he knew a gap in the market. Most people of his acquaintance could get knock-off cigarettes in The Crown at vastly-reduced prices. They were usually stolen or made by people who didn't mind adding something illegal or poisonous to the product. But Don knew others who weren't allowed in pubs. Their presence would lead to bar staff running from behind the counter brandishing something sharp or heavy or both.

That demographic was Don's clientele. There was something poor and something interesting about these people. The festivities weren't the best time for them so that increased demand.

His main problem was he now had opposition. Thomasina - it just didn't sound right for this line of work—had access to superior quality papers. Word was some were Christmas-themed. Don fretted. Would they be green and red or even flavoured? Seasonal alternatives to liquorice paper. Christmas pudding tabs or roast turkey and stuffing tabs. Mulled wine tabs. Or Boxing Day cigar tabs. That could be a winner. Cigar-flavoured cigarettes. A rich man's pleasure at a poor man's price. He could see the billboards. He could play both characters. He'd wear that fancy dressing gown his mam had bought him for the rich man, and he'd wear what he was wearing for the poor man.

He sniffed and started breaking up. Filters and scraps of paper in a Heron carrier bag. Tobacco in a large brown mixing bowl he'd once used for making bread with Cheryl. He wore the disposable gloves he'd taken from Morrison's petrol station before being shouted at. He considered the shades from puce yellow to cack brown and summoned up positive feelings.

He started to feel proud. He was going to do something special. Ideas started to form. He had some lining paper under his bed and he had Cheryl's blackboard paint.

He spent the day carefully painting. He'd leave a part or layer to dry, then return to the tabs. In his head he'd tweak some details about the advertising campaign.

The following morning he had glue on his hands and a rare feeling of satisfaction. It wasn't the best billboard in the world, but it was his.

Onion

Damhnait Monaghan

When I get home from the supermarket, she's sitting in the kitchen, a small brown suitcase at her feet. Our eyes meet. I hold on tight to that connection, until she looks away.

"Mum," she says. "Don't try to stop me."

I sling the burlap shopping bag on the table and an onion rolls out. She reaches to stop it from falling to the floor and I flinch at the sight of that pale thin arm. Put a jumper on, I want to scream. I walk to the sink and fill the kettle. I know how this goes. In the few minutes I have left with her, we'll drink coffee and she'll tell me how this time it will be different.

This time he's got a job. Or his own flat. Look, he gave me this necklace.

We both jump at the short sharp bleat of the horn outside. They never come to the door, never ring the bell. She gives me a too quick hug and slams the door behind her.

I grab a knife from the drawer and reach for the onion. The tears won't come on their own.

My Aunt Maggie
Paul McVeigh

My Aunt Maggie's house smells. Her breath does too. Her biscuits are always soggy and they're never chocolate. That's cuz she's poor. She's poorer than Colm Mulvenna in my class who has sugar sandwiches for lunch every day. My Aunt Maggie always has bruises. Cuz she never does anything right. That's what my Uncle Malachy says. But my Uncle Malachy doesn't know anything. My Aunt Maggie is the best! She sings me songs and dances with me too. She holds my hands and we run in a circle and shout *Yoo hoo!* and we laugh and laugh till we hold our stomachs and fall onto the settee.

My Aunt Maggie is quiet and she's always busy. Moving ornaments and straightening pictures and wiping under cups when there's nothing there to wipe. She never sits her fat arse down. Getting on everybody's fucking nerves. That's what Uncle Malachy says. But she doesn't when she's on her own with me.

You only have to look at my Aunt Maggie to know all she wants is to be happy. And for everybody to be happy together. And I know. I know. I know this is true. For definite. Not cuz she's told me. I see it in every wipe. And I know it, with all of the tingles on my arm, because I want that too. But there's only us that does. Nobody else. So I hide it. And so does she.

But not when she's on her own with me.

I'm going to tell you a secret. I've never told anyone this before. When we're on our own, my Aunt Maggie holds me in her arms. And she hugs me. Tight to her. And doesn't let go. And I never want her to. I want to stay there until I die. We die. Together.

And today, right, today, she says to me, she says, 'Stephen son,' she says, 'Stephen son, I – love – you.'

And I'm not making it up. I didn't see it on the TV or anything. My Aunt Maggie loves me, me, me. She does. She does. She does. And I know. I know. I know. Because when she said those words to me my heart hurt and my eyes stung and I felt so sick, my stomach tried to leave me and go to her and stay with her forever cuz I can't. I wish Aunt Maggie was my Mummy. I wish I'd grown inside her tummy and that I could remember being held by her all day long. I wish she'd leave Uncle Malachy and take me with her. We could run away together. When I grow up I can marry her and it doesn't matter that she will be older than me because she's older than me now and it doesn't.

I'll keep her safe. I'll never, ever hurt her. And she'll give me hugs and say those words to me every day. And we'll be happy forever and ever.

A Box of Stars Beneath the Bed
Jon Stubbington

The box was a gift on our seventh date. It was small and made of wood. On each side an engraving, so worn that I couldn't make out the pictures. One might have been an elephant. Then again, it might not. "It's lovely," I said, feeling the smooth ridges of its surface. "Open it," Steven replied, smiling, excited. There was no clasp or clip, just a hinged lid. I slid a fingernail into the crack underneath and gently opened the top. Inside it was vast. Deep and black and filled with a million million stars. I looked inside and felt myself a god, or an ant: so big and yet so tiny. It was everything and it was beautiful. "Well?" he asked, expectant, hopeful. I stared at the stars that swirled slowly through the immense open space inside. "It's beautiful," I said, "and unbelievable. It's the most amazing thing I have ever seen."

"It's for you." Galaxies twirled and turned, spinning through the small wooden box in my hands. It was everything and he had given it to me. "Thank you," I said. It didn't seem enough.

The box lived in our lounge, on a shelf beside the books. We would take it down once, twice, three times a day. Steven would sit beside me to open it, to stare into its depths, and to marvel at its magic. Stars spun, twinkling in the darkness. It was everything.

We neglected our jobs, forgot our friends; we began to slide away from the world. *This is silly*, we said. *We must be better than this.* So we imposed limits: once a day, that was all. Together, each evening. Steven and me and the box.

"I'm going to move it," Steven said, holding the box. "Move it where? Why?" "Mother won't like it," he said. "Why not?" I asked. "It is magical and beautiful; something so special that it demands to be seen. We should shout about it from the rooftops, force our friends to come and see it, stop strangers in the street." "She will think it's showy. She doesn't like that sort of thing." "It's a box full of stars: a universe we can hold in our hands. It shouldn't be and yet it is. It transcends space and time." "I know," he said. "But can it transcend space and time somewhere else instead?"

The box now lives beneath the bed. Although we look at it less often than once we did, it comforts me to know it's there.

Sometimes, when it is dark outside and the other stars are circling above us, we will take it out and open its lid. We stare at it in wonder and we remember that it is everything. It is beautiful.

Sometimes we will fall asleep with galaxies turning between us. Sometimes it sits beneath us: closed, waiting.

But it is always there, and it is everything and it is beautiful.

A Collection

Diane Simmons

I throw in the opal ring next. It makes little impression on the river, unlike the jade bracelet and the gold chain I bought in Marrakech.

The opal ring had been the start of my collection, bought just a week after Sophie was born. 'Something for me,' I'd reasoned, as gift after gift arrived for her.

The last piece I select is my mother's engagement ring. It's a diamond cluster, the only decent jewellery she'd owned. When she died, I cried as I surveyed the cheap beads and mean -stoned rings I'd inherited. It didn't seem much to show for a life.

So I'd started collecting – birthdays, Christmases, anniversaries, I asked my husband for jewellery, determined that Sophie would have an inheritance to delight in.

As soon as she took an interest, I allowed her to play with the cheaper pieces, let her rummage in my wardrobe for heels and hats to parade in. As she grew older, she borrowed necklaces for university balls, rings for friends' weddings, brooches for job interviews. 'Can I keep the sapphire ring?' she often begged. 'Or the opal?'

'You can have them when I'm dead,' I used to say.

So stupid. I should have showered my beautiful girl with everything I owned. Not carried on building a collection that would never be needed.

As I trudge back to the car, I look down at my left hand, twirl the ring on my middle finger. It's a ruby, antique, bought as a present for Sophie's graduation. She'd been so proud of her First and she adored the ring, had rarely taken it off. It doesn't look good on me. But I didn't hesitate when the undertaker handed it to me. I slipped it on to my finger, have kept it there ever since. It's the only jewellery I have now, the only piece I see any point in owning.

Kelly Loves Traffic Light Jelly

Jeanette Sheppard

The supermarket man has moved the jelly higher up. I can't see the pictures on the packets now. Mum says we don't have time to stop for jelly anyway — we have to buy Nina's present. Kelly rhymes with Jelly. Every Tuesday after school Dad used to say, 'Let's make Traffic Light Jelly, Kelly.' Dad was the man who made all the bulbs for the traffic lights for all the streets in our town.

Nina's got jelly at her party. It's not Traffic Light Jelly though. Traffic Light Jelly is red, yellow and green. First it smells of strawberries, then lemons, then limes. Nina's party jelly is pink and smells of violets, but that's okay — Mum says we all like different things. Dad said we have to make jelly properly though. I tell Nina her party jelly doesn't wobble properly. Mum is walking up from the bottom of the garden with Nina's mum. Nina's mum is showing Mum the new garden full of fluffy flowers. Mum doesn't like flowers, but she is saying 'they are lovely.' When they go past us Nina kicks me in the shin. I yelp. Mum turns. Her mouth does an O when she sees the muddy boot mark on Nina's pink ballerina skirt and Nina rubbing her eyes. Mum rushes up to me. She tells me to say sorry. I say sorry. She takes my hand and says, 'I think it's best if we go.' Nina's mum does one of those sing-songy looks people do a lot now Dad's not here, with her neck stuck on one side.

In the car Mum says, 'What did you say, Kelly? Were you talking about Traffic Light Jelly again?' I shake my head. Nina's mum hadn't made proper jelly. It was supposed to wobble, but it slipped off my spoon. I want to tell Mum that jelly has to be left in the fridge for ages. Nina's dad doesn't make jelly either. Dad made the best jelly. Dad made Traffic Light Jelly for my party. My party jelly was the best ever. Mum stops at the traffic lights. The lights go red, red yellow, yellow, green. You are supposed to go now, but Mum doesn't drive off. She just stares at the green light.

Yellow
Nuala Ní Chonchúir

At the entrance, a woman hands each of us a net. When I imagined this moment, I saw us being given a single net. We would move as one, four hands on the handle, catching our baby together.

'Twice the chance,' Rob hisses, snapping the net like a riding crop.

Yes, I think, *yes*. Double the opportunity. One hundred per cent better. Yes, yes!

We run side by side down the corridor, with all the other hopefuls, into the dome. I see babies high in the roof space, they helicopter and dive. The air smells of talc and scalp. A Pink with putto thighs flies towards me and I shove past a man and try to net her. She dodges upwards and skims sideways. I jump high, knocking against the man again, but I miss.

'Get fucked!' the man screams at me and chases the Pink, arcing his net wildly but it meets empty air.

Up ahead I see Rob dip his net under a drifting Blue.

'Stop!' I shout, waving my arms. We agreed Pink and the rules are clear: one baby per couple. If Rob snags a Blue, it is over. 'What the hell are you at?' Rob steps back from the Blue and holds his palms out in surrender. 'Pink,' I snarl.

Then I see it, executing a cocky glissade above all the Pinks and Blues – a Yellow. Its face is turtlish but it looks strong. It seems unconcerned as it streels across the dome, surveying the waggle of a hundred nets and the anxiety of the would-be parents below. I catch the Yellow's eye and it holds my gaze.

'Come to me,' I whisper. Keeping watch on its robust body, I see it gravitate towards me. The Yellow's eyes are clear and bright; it stares at me as if in recognition. I lift my net then let it fall to the floor. I open my arms and the Yellow descends, poised as a hawk.

The baby snuggles its head to my breast and Rob is

suddenly at my side, placing his hand respectfully on the little one's beautiful head. We look at each other and smile. We look back at the baby. Our golden child. Our Yellow.

First published online at Cease, Cows (http://ceasecows.com/2014/04/18/yellow-by-nuala-ni-chonchuir/)

424 Likes
Jennifer Harvey

Today she posted a new picture. Between morning and afternoon it gathered 424 likes, the little red heart gleaming and boastful. At one point I even thought I saw it pulsate as it basked in the warm glow of admiration, like it was taunting me. She was taunting me.

'424 likes. In three hours. 424. 424. 424. Thump, thump, thump. You'd never manage that.'

It's true, I wouldn't. It's a competition I can never win and I stopped trying months ago. 'I don't like what it's doing to me,' is what I told her when I closed my account.

Also true. I didn't like what it was doing to me. The way it made me look at her and think: 'Why her? Why does she get to be so special?'

But she misunderstood, linked her arm through mine and let her head fall against my shoulder, tried to ease my insecurities. 'It's real friends that count,' she told me. 'A buncha likes online means nothing.'

An hour later, she posted a new photo. The two of us together. She's smiling and I'm trying my best to. #BFF she tagged it.

Every time her phone pinged she would brandish it. 'Hey, we got another like.' But later, when I logged in at home I saw all the comments were about her. No-one asked who the BFF was.

Save for this one girl. Everyone calls her 'Kitty' because her avatar is a Persian cat, all fluffy and white just like the one that James Bond villain had.

'Who's the plain Jane?' she asked.

'Hey that's my best friend!' came the reply and I have to admit it came back quickly. I mean, she defended me.

'Kitty' apologised too. 'A bit of make-up and she could look okay is all I mean.'

No reply. Which left the comment hanging there like a statement of fact. So now Kitty is becoming bolder. Polite still, nice still, but with a hint of claw.

A gold sequinned top is, 'Amazing! So glam! But maybe just a bit too harsh for your skin tone?'

A new bobbed hairstyle is admired, 'So sleek and chic! I think no shorter than the chin line works better for your bone structure though.'

It's a drip, drip, drip designed to undermine her self-confidence.

And it's working. The day after that haircut I saw her tucking her hair behind her ears, then pulling it back again. Over and over.

I almost purred with pleasure as I watched her fidget.

I log on. Click like and watch the total rise to 425.

'Oh magenta is *the* colour this autumn! Really suits you.'

'Thanks!' she pings back.

'It's everywhere though, eh? Think I'm going to go for burgundy, just to be a little bit different, you know?'

No reply. But I know I scratched her just then. I know she'll never wear that blouse again. 'Meouw' I type. Though I don't send it. I just hit delete and smile.

Manspreading
Marie Gethins

Amy knew how to judge men. Sweet, salty, sour, pungent, astringent, bitter. At first, it took several dates: stilted chatter, a few deep sniffs, a brief tongue dance. By twenty-eight, she honed the process. She hovered near a prospect for a minute or two and took in their aroma. Her friends accused her of being fickle, but Amy enjoyed the taster menu. 'Who wants the same thing every day?' she asked other girls. Yet even she grew weary of shopping around bars and bistros, scanning available male stock at the gym. As a scientist, she wondered if biochemistry might offer a solution.

She scoured documents for potential methods. East German secret police had developed the technique, but Amy perfected it. Capturing someone's scent, then concentrating, fermenting, and storing the essence. A straightforward process and with the availability of component volatiles on the web, quite simple to reproduce. The food base proved trickier.

Amy enrolled in night classes at the local culinary institute. She learned the foundations of gourmet cuisine—lump-free roux, clear broth, smooth pastes. Long-life food storage research followed. After six months of diligence and exhaustive romantic interludes, her cabinet and freezer featured a broad collection.

One night friends dragged Amy to a new restaurant opening. From a corner booth they surveyed the buffet seated at other tables or lingering near the bar. 'Oh, he looks yummy,' one said, pointing to a handsome jock. 'Tom?' Amy smiled. 'Nice spread on white toast, but insipid if combined with anything stronger.'

Wake Up
Oli Morriss

It was a long time since your neighbours saw you as anything other than the man with a coat of lightbulbs. A carnival-esque figure who never laughed or smiled or spoke. Some people began to think you didn't exist. Some people thought you were dead. But everyone knew you had a coat of lightbulbs.

They took your son.

It has been a long time since you've left the house, your sustenance coming from carers with plastic smiles and meals-on-wheels and neighbours who "accidentally made an extra cake and I thought you might like it" but just wanted to get a glimpse of your coat.

You went to sleep and they took your son.

You open the door like you have done every day for the last 15 years and slowly raise your foot across the threshold. If anyone had cared to watch they would've thought it sad and sighed and tutted and shaken their heads, but to you it was a victory. Every day you can feel yourself getting further out, closer to putting your foot down on the creaking wooden steps. You long for that day.

It was dark and you went to sleep and they took your son.

You go back inside and shuffle towards the living room and look at your coat of lightbulbs on its stand. They'll never catch you unawares again. Never.

You obeyed your orders when it was dark and you went to sleep and they took your son.

You take the coat and wrap yourself in it. It jingles slightly, but the glass is muffled against the fabric and is soon quiet again. You sit on a stool and face the doorway to the living room.

They cut the fuse and you obeyed your orders when it was dark and you went to sleep and they took your son.

The lightbulbs glow and even through the thick fabric

holding them together they burn your skin, powered in a mockery of your rage. Your rage. Your choice.

They took your son.
It was him or you.

When Dreams are Large and Tusked
Ingrid Jendrzejewski

She wishes that magical things would happen in her stories. Somehow, her writing always ends up being about everyday things like family life and the goings on in small towns. These are not the kinds of stories she likes reading, however. She prefers books about unusual things like disappearing elephants and giant insects who were once salesmen. These sorts of things never seem to manifest in her work. She asks herself why this might be and is mystified.

One day, she is writing at the kitchen table, ignoring the dishes stacked up by the sink. She has a glass of wine to hand, which makes her feel a little braver than usual. She decides she will no longer stand for it. She tells herself that she is in control of her stories; there is no reason something out of the ordinary shouldn't happen in one. It's up to her. So, with resolve and a heady sense of adventure, she plops a walrus right smack dab in the middle of the story that she is writing.

At first she is elated; something extraordinary is finally happening. However, her enthusiasm soon begins to fade; the walrus doesn't seem to be doing anything interesting, nor does it seem to be very engaged in her story. She had not thought very carefully about the reality of walruses; now she is realizing that the creature smells terrible and makes the most disconcerting grunts and whistles. It fills her kitchen with its violent, thrashing flippers and brandishes its tusks whenever she dares to look in its direction.

She is not sure what to do with the walrus. In the end, it doesn't help her story at all, and now that she's finally ready to do the dishes, she finds that it's in the way.

Ten Things that Happened After My Funeral

Santino Prinzi

1. I realised I was in purgatory and didn't know what to do, so I finished my dissertation and other deadlines for my degree. They'll never be marked. Kind words were said about me at graduation by my supervisor. People who disliked me told everyone how wonderful they thought I was. I laughed, Mum wept.

2. When I discovered my boyfriend had been cheating on me for months, I haunted his lover. He adored books, which surprised me because my boyfriend always complained how I'd buy more books than we had space for. But there was space for his lover's books, despite his poor taste, so I did them both a favour and tore the books up. My boyfriend got the blame and they're not together now, but I still didn't feel any better.

3. I became a superhero. I saved lives using a method I'd perfected in life: I got in everyone's way. Don't thank the stiff door or the keys you couldn't find – thank me. Death soon caught on and he wasn't impressed. "You can't do that. It's their time." "But it wasn't mine when you took me." "You don't decide that."

4. I tried all the things I was too scared to do when alive, but being dead removed any risk and made everything that unexciting. You try sky diving without gravity…

5. My mum died. It was upsetting, but I was happy to spend some quality time together. She soon had to leave for Heaven, against both our wills. "I have the final say," Death told us both. Saying goodbye was worse than dying.

6. I was angry with Death. I wanted him to take notice, so I tore down the Golden Gate Bridge during rush hour. Lots of people died; I know I should be sorry but I'm not. Incidentally, I avoid San Francisco now.

7. Death called me into his office and told me I needed to go on a soul-searching mission. "How do I know when I'm finished? I assume I'm a soul myself?" Death shrugged his shoulders. "When you'll know, you'll know."

8. I explored the entire world, every inch, crevice, depth. I could've cheated: I could've floated through the air, or even through the Earth's crust. Instead I walked. Hundreds of years passed. I saw it all and more.

9. I found my place in the world: The Sahara Desert. There's something beautiful about the eerie stillness that appealed to me. You can sit for years and listen. It's helped me let everything go, though I still don't know why I'm here.

10. Death called me back to his office. He wasn't there but I went inside. On his desk was his scythe and his black robe folded neatly in a small pile. I didn't need to read the note.

What the Therapist Said
Jude Higgins

I was floating naked in a mountain pool when he flew overhead in his paraglider. A Greek god, finding his way to earth.

'I knew it would be you,' he said later, when I picked him up at the roadside. 'It's destiny.'

In the beginning, we were happy. He said the sex blew him away. For me, it was like being swept in a current so powerful, I had to let go or drown. But in his city high-rise, I wouldn't venture on to the balcony. At my riverside flat, he felt the damp and longed for pure mountain air.

It was the couples' therapist who summed us up.

'A fish might love a bird, but where would they live?' she said.

While I mopped up my tears, he stretched out his arms as if they were wings.

We parted.

Now, every time I look at the sky, I'm searching for him and in the water, however much I love to swim, I'm no longer in my element.

Gregor Samsa Quits the Track Team
Beverly C. Lucey

When Greg woke up from a dream in which he couldn't run anymore, he found that overnight he had become stuck on his bed. His heels hurt as if he had been pushing down on them for hours. Thinking he'd had a stroke he tried taking the FAST steps. He could only make one side of his mouth move; his arms felt like limp noodles. Could he call for help? A scratchy sound, like the ones from his grandmother's old Victrola, came from his blistering throat. No one could help because his bedroom door was locked.

Why had he locked the door? Because he would wake too often to find his mother standing over him, sighing. Sometimes she would sit on his bed and whimper about her meager life. He had to get some sleep.

His father had been let go from his foreman's job months ago. When Greg told his coach he was quitting school and the track team because he had to work, the coach had looked at him with contempt instead of pity. Still, Greg did it for the family. They needed him and the money he brought home. He would call 911 but could not reach his phone on the night table.

He could tell the sun was high in the sky from the warm light angle at his window. His parents should have got him up for his job at the mill hours ago. His mother cried all the time. His father yelled at everything. Ginger, his useless sister, spent her time in front of mirrors, waiting for rescue in that fairy tale mind of hers. He must get up.

A few hours later, Greg had maneuvered to the side of his bed with his heels and one elbow that had become more bone than noodle. Then he rocked himself onto the floor but was now wedged between the bed and window.

At the sound, his parents pounded at his door. Ginger

picked the lock, one of her few talents, and all three came tumbling into the room.

"Where is that bum?" roared his father. His mother moaned when she found Greg on the floor. "Call the doctor," Ginger said. "No!" screamed his father. "We don't have insurance. People like us, no one cares."

For weeks they made do. His mother discovered that the state would pay them to take care of Greg at home. It was the cheapest way. Checks came that were bigger than Greg's mill salary. Mother stopped crying. His father could buy beer again. Ginger would bring him leftovers and feed Greg by hand. Then she forgot. She forgot for a week, then another, and she was the only one who ever went into the room.

When she remembered, Greg was long dead. Ginger dragged him to a closet and put old clothes over him. When her parents asked about him month to month, Ginger shrugged and said, "He's the same way he's been." The checks kept coming. Life was better.

Honesty's Not the Best Policy
Brendan Way

'Izzy, I know this is only our third date, but I want you to have this.' Zach slides a wad of paper across the table.

'What is it?'

'It's a list of my habits. My quirks. My non-negotiable views. All stuff you'd learn within six months anyway but I thought I'd skip ahead and lay out all my cards.'

Zach did not blink once during that explanation. Izzy picks up the pack.

'I-'

'Look. I've been round the relationship block a few times. I'm just trying to save us some time.'

'By admitting upfront that...' Izzy skims through the first page, 'you won't give to the homeless because 'they're blatantly all on drugs'?'

'I'm just calling it as I see it! We don't have to agree on everything to be compatible...'

A discontented 'hmm' from Izzy. She flips over another sheet.

'You don't call your dad – you wait for him to ring?'

'Cos I'm the alpha.' Zach tears into a piece of bread, stuffs it into his mouth. 'So, is there anything you'd like to share?'

'Uh... sure.' Riiip. Scribble scribble. She slides over a tiny piece of paper. Zach picks it up.

'"I hate you'.'

Izzy nods.

'That's great! Real breakthrough, babe. Let's take this to couples counselling next week!'

His pack hits him in the face as Izzy storms out. Zach laughs.

'Running out before paying? I love doing that! It's on page four...'

Orphans
Chris Stanley

Billy's linen shirt is buttoned up all wrong and he's still wearing his 'seven today' badge from the previous weekend. He sniffs cautiously at the yellowed grains on the plate in front of him and the fart smell of boiled egg and smoked fish makes him wince. What have they ordered this time? The waiter places the exact same dish in front of Kate and Nathan but they're too busy thumbing their phones to notice. Behind them, the horizon rises and falls as the giant cruise ship slow-bounces towards Marseilles or Monte Carlo or whichever Mediterranean port they're invading today. Billy pokes at his breakfast with his fork.

'What's this?' he asks.

Kate looks up, her mouth an O of annoyance. 'It's kedgeree. You won't like it, sweetie. I thought you wanted cereal?'

'Just eat it,' says Nathan. 'It's good for you.' Nathan ordered the food.

'It does look yummy,' says Billy. Kate and Nathan used to laugh when he was silly but now they call it sarcasm and sarcasm isn't helpful.

Using his fork, Billy imagines he's a tornado and whips the kedgeree around his plate with increasing speed until flecks of curried rice go flying across the table. He stops, expecting to be told off, but Kate and Nathan are so engrossed in their phones they hardly know they're eating.

'Look at this,' says Kate. 'Spinal muscular atrophy. She wasn't supposed to see her first birthday and now she's about to turn four. How amazing.'

'You want to send money?' asks Nathan. 'Or petition for better healthcare?'

'It just says to send a card.'

'We'll send money.'

Every mealtime, it's the same thing. Billy sits in silence while Kate and Nathan prod the corners of the internet in search of some physically or socially malnourished child they can help rescue from a life of misery. Orphans are their favourites because every child deserves to be loved and they can transfer their love using PayPal.

'Have we sent anything to the kids in Calais this week?' asks Nathan.

Billy remembers the pictures of the Syrian boy lying face down on a Turkish beach. Kate tried to stop him seeing them but it was already too late. The clothes upset Billy the most, the red T-shirt and trainers. Real people wear clothes. Kate cuddled him on the sofa and tried to explain while Nathan wept at the horror of it all. Before the Syrian boy, Billy felt like he was the centre of their world. Afterwards, all they talked about was how they could make the world a better place.

Back in the restaurant, with the luxury liner slowing down on approach to Santorini or Argostoli or wherever, Kate says 'What about Meningitis B vaccines for all children?'

Billy slips off his chair.

'You going to the playroom, buddy?' asks Nathan.

'I'm going to jump overboard.'

'Do you need money for that?'

When Billy doesn't answer, both parents look up from their phones but their son is already gone.

And the Red Flower

Nina Lindmark Lie

I usually saw nothing. Same old route, to the same old place, and on the way there was rarely something new. And then, there was a little red flower. It grew in the dark earth, sprouting tender leaves all coated with frost. The sheets of ice lay on the petals and smothered the aroma yet captured its beauty for all to see. The struggle of something small, was what I saw, as I waited at the bus stop—while the cold touched my cheeks and frosted the tips of my hair. It glistened like a candied apple at the fair, thin and sweet, and I could feel the taste of it, the texture of it, on my tongue. Fleeting thoughts. The bus came, I left, and the ground thawed.

One Last Pickup
Sarah Hilary

The first was a flat tyre. Tim rolled up in good time, wrench in hand, smile in place. 'Knights of the Road.'

She laughed with relief. In her forties, bottle-blonde highlights. Hint of desperation that predated, he guessed, the roadside recovery. High heels snagged at the tarmac as she watched him work. He got her going again, all right.

The second one was a dead battery. Tim gave his best salute. 'Riding to the rescue.'

Who could resist a gent with a sense of humour?

She was Clare, that one. Hard shoulder, soft top.

When Rita asked how his day went, Tim said, 'Terrific.'

She tapped her fingers on the table. Painted nails, metallic-finish. Tough customer, his wife. Not a whiff of the damsel in distress about Rita.

Number three? A faulty fan-belt.' Pop the lid for me would you, love?'

He wouldn't have risked the 'love' but she was old enough to be his mum and they both knew it. Proper little goer, though. Lola, believe it or not.

Five and six were twins. It didn't get much better. 'Your rear end's gone,' Tim told them. 'I'm sorry to say.'

He felt like James Bond, no brakes, touching 80mph.

The roads melted; Summer heatwave. Tim tackled overheated engines, got under the bonnet so often he lost count, topped up the oil, deployed his dipstick. A rare old time.

Rita said, 'You want to recharge your own battery for a change.'

Bitch. He'd never any trouble getting it up at the roadside. Maybe it was the open air, bitter-sweet smell of bitumen and burning fossil fuels, his role in the rescues. He loved to hear,

'Lone female breakdown,' 'Stranded,' 'Priority'. A chance to play the old-fashioned hero, get chivalrous.

This one was wearing driving shoes, the kind with the rubber treads underneath. Sensible. Decent set of legs on her. Dash of makeup, not as much as he liked. 'Hope you weren't waiting too long,' he said.

'You were very quick.' She had a great smile.

Middle of nowhere. Perfect spot for it.

'I'm Tim, by the way.'

'Diana.'

'Let's get the bonnet up and see what's causing the trouble, shall we?'

She sat in the driver's seat, sprang the lid.

Tim had a quick rummage. Never saw the wrench coming. Just heard the rev of speeding air, and the words, 'From Rita, with love.'

First published in M.O. Crimes of Practice *by Comma Press in 2008.*

Sunday Morning
John Holland

My mother and father had sexual intercourse every Sunday morning at 9.00. As a teenager I listened in bed to the steady rhythm of their love making with a mixture of fascination and revulsion. It reminded me of the slow night train from Keighley to Pudsey, its regular tempo unfaltering, almost hypnotic. Except, of course, that my parents didn't scream to a halt every ten minutes to let more people on.

My dad applied the same rhythm to all practical matters. Digging the ground in the back garden; inflating the blow-up bed with a foot pump when camping; or chipping potatoes for tea. He was unhurried and purposeful, calm and steady - with the desired result fully in his grasp.

It never occurred to me to enter into a conversation over breakfast about what I had heard.

"I bet that's given you an appetite, our mum."

Or,

"Is your physical love a manifestation of your emotional bond, dear parents?"

Or,

"Has dad always been a sex machine?"

No, it was not spoken of. After all, it was a private matter. Well, almost private.

My own experiences at the time were more clandestine. When a girlfriend stayed over on Saturday night we were given separate rooms. But, this being the 1960s, the girl would expect me to share her bed at some point. If I was not forthcoming, she, as a Yorkshire girl, was entitled, under the Huddersfield Sexual Convention of 1963, to refer to me as "Old Tired Balls". Or, on one occasion, to describe me as being, and I quote here, "more interested in your tropical fish than fellatio."

When I was able to put my cichlids and sucking catfish to

the back of my mind, the night-time would usually find me bed hopping. And when the sun rose, my parents' 9am Sunday ritual provided a further opportunity for young love, as we knew we would not be caught at this time.

One Sunday morning, as well as my girlfriend, my sister and her new husband stayed over. At 9.00 all three couples were at it simultaneously. I wondered if Bonnie and Ronnie, our Dutch rabbits, in the hutch by the back door, were also making love amongst the straw and droppings. And in the aquarium in the lounge were the tropical fish - the mollies, guppies and platies - flexing their gonopodia and partaking in their own watery way?

Was it possible that the neighbours could actually see our house rocking? Definitely not, because on this particular day, the house was rendered completely invisible by an emerging fog of serotonin, prolactin and oxytocin. In fact, such was its density, that a cumulo-nimbus formed above the house, resulting in us having our own microclimate.

On that day, it literally rained love.

About Unemployment and Rats
Bernard O'Rourke

I walked the eleven steps to the bottom of our back garden and stood there looking for odd birds or clouds that I could tell you about when you got home from work. I heard the sound of our neighbours (to the right) making love – "I want you," herself was yelling, "I want you to fuck me." Their bedroom is at the front, just like ours, so my theory is they were at it in that back room with the washing machine. They lasted long enough for our dinner to burn. I'd planned to surprise you with a lamb casserole (w/ red wine and herbs). There were chips too. Now there are little inky strips of charcoal. They look like drowned rats washed up on a beach.

"Rats?" You standing in the doorway: puzzled facial expression and Chinese takeaway bags.

"The chips look a bit like—"

Hands raised means stop speaking. You don't need to hear me explain the reason for my distraction. "Stop trying to cook, baby. You're really shit at it." But I cooked because there was leftover wine. And you wouldn't understand the type of things a half-consumed bottle says to me in the early afternoon.

Captain Strix

Zoe Gilbert

The owl rig hangs over the forest. A gigantic black insect, its legs scuff the oak canopy.

There are legends:

It used to be manned, by a crew in tin hats and goggles.

It used to bear one man, Captain Strix, who swept pellets from its dark edges with his broom and slept on a heap of feathers.

It has never been manned, and is steered by the owls themselves, with levers adapted for talons.

Believe what you like.

Why the rig has legs at all is a subject of speculation. Nobody is sure when it launched. A reckless tree climber once sprang for it, vaulting from a beech bough to hang like a Gortex-ed spider from one of the iron feet. He was dislodged, they say, when the rig swung through 180 degrees and gave a screech that was heard a mile away. His body lay draped in a hornbeam nook for a week before he was found.

And why our forest? The owl rig is a blot on the skyscape. Our houses are plagued by refugee mice.

In my bungalow, where the small garden abuts the forest, the mice line up on the window sills on full moon nights, to squeak at the horror movie beyond the glass. The sweep of taut wing, the furious dive; death among the rhododendrons. Once, the soulless glow of two eyes, right there above the sun lounger. The mice shudder but do not flee when the rig sails close, blocking out the moon. We wouldn't be without it.

The rig is old now. It creaks and lurches, dumping feathers in filthy drifts. Does it hang lower over the forest, weighed down by strata of pellets and guano? How many owls now roost in its ironwork?

There are conjectures:

It will come gently to ground, soon, landing on its rusty legs.

It will crash, in a scream of twisted metal, amongst the trees.

It will vanish, and our mice will return to their tree trunk homes in a frenzy of spring cleaning.

Believe what you like.

I've begun my own spring cleaning, though I spare the nests of shredded paper that rustle in the corners of my bungalow. The mice watch, twitching their whiskers as I empty out the broom cupboard and dust off the tin hat and goggles. In the garden, I give them a wash and leave them to dry on the lawn. I shake out the broom, scattering old feathers and tiny bones into the grass. I don't wish to frighten my lodgers.

When the moon rises tonight, I'll leave the back door open while I walk into the forest. My tin hat will gleam in the silver light as I climb the oak that stands highest. I'll listen for the rig to come clanking, hooting, a hundred owls dragging it towards its final voyage.

Latchkey
Fiona J. Mackintosh

"It's catch as catch can tonight," says Mum, easel under her arm, slapping the strewn newspapers for her keys. I look up from *Bleak House.*
"Supper?"
"A clever invention called sandwiches."
"Very droll, Mother."
"There's cheese. And lettuce."
She kisses Jerome's head. Finger's up his nose as usual.
"Later, bunnies. Don't set any fires."
Car door slams. I'm with Esther and Mr. Bucket galloping through the snow in search of Lady Dedham. I turn the pages faster under the lamp's circle. Just as Esther lifts the veil from the dead woman's face, I hear something.
"Jerome?"
Cellar door's open, steps vanishing into darkness.
"I know you're down there."
No sound.
"Stop pretending this minute." The silence is soupy, dense.
"I'm making supper. You better come."
Bread knife in hand, I lean the book against the toaster and step back into the black hole that yawns between the pages.

Lips
Nik Perring

When the thin-lipped man and the stout-lipped woman met and fell in love there was always going to be trouble. Even you might wonder what they could possibly have been thinking. But they did meet and they did fall in love, and that's a fact.

And so it began. And it began well.

Mr Thin-lips fell in love with Mrs Stout-lips completely. With the tight curls of her hair, with the way she spoke – so softly - even with the way she'd sigh sadly at the most insignificant of things. But most of all he fell in love with her mouth. He loved how her top lip rose like a wave, and he loved how it felt against him – warm and cushioned, safe and lovely.

And she, Mrs Stout-lips, she loved him back and she loved *his* mouth too. She loved how it fitted perfectly with hers, how it felt like the key that unlocked her.

So, in the beginning, where all this began, their mouths were smiles, one full and plump, the other neat and slim. When they weren't pressed against each other, of course. There was a lot of pressing in the beginning.

But, before long, something terrible happened. Mrs Stout-lips noticed it first and when she did she thought: No! It can't be!

But it was.

Mr Thin-lips' lips felt wider to her. They felt fuller. There was simply more of them.

But it was he who, weeks later, said, 'Darling, I may be imagining this, but I think your lips are shrinking.'

They stood next to each other in front of her bathroom mirror.

'I've noticed it too,' she admitted with a sigh, and they held each other's hands as they peered into that mirror, and they squeezed tightly as they stepped forward to take a closer look.

Those reflections, those two worried faces, stared back at them and they simply could not deny it. It was right in front them and it was cruel.

It was as though their lips had grown and shrunk at almost exactly the same rate because now they were almost exactly the same size.

'What are we to do?' they said, at almost exactly the same time. And though neither replied, they both knew. So they held each other, and as he held her he thought of waves, and as she held him she thought of keys, but neither of them smiled, and neither of them sighed, they just stood there, and waited.

Map Reading

Jane Roberts

The man who maps your heart is a traveller; although he doesn't know about cartography and all that he inspires. Yet. If he looked back to see you following him right now, you know he would not understand your bearings, your pilgrimage.

You journey together for miles, leagues. The words and silences and latitudes and longitudes guide you, close you together like an Ordnance Survey map folding up its weary concertina spine; a map complete in places, incomplete – and aching for compass point – in others. Distance between you – or lack of it – becomes a matter of sentiment, not logic…not mathematics.

This is the way. This is the way neither of you have taken before.

How to Make Lolo
Michelle Elvy

Fun comes in large doses round here, babes swinging in tyres, boys climbing wrecked hulls, girls excavating hermit crabs. Your Carolina towhead's right at home among these island kids. You've been here one month now but it may as well be three or four. Time has stopped. Everything is different. He is gone, swallowed silently and forever by the swirling Pacific. Not a trace of his life was found. Not a single piece of clothing, not a molecule—though you suppose his atoms are currently reforming from solid to liquid to gas. Absorbed, universal.

Your girl glances up from the water's edge, flips her hand like a small fish, back and forth, back and forth. Wet, slippery, shiny. Pretty against the bright Fijian sky. Her baby teeth flash, too. Each year, she will look more like him. You can see her cowlick from here, errant hair standing at attention from her small head. Like his. You wave back though your arm feels heavy. The other kids all wave now: a game. Swish, swish go their brown hands, flashing against the backdrop of sea and sky.

Why did you stay? Why aren't you back home with family, school, alarm clocks? With paved roads leading the way to and fro, lines marking a clear direction and traffic lights blinking *Stop, Go*?

You sit on the low porch, grating coconut with Kalesi, knees gripping the large bowl. You follow her expert strokes, her strong arms, wanting to do it just right. As if there is order in these small tasks. Order and the promise of something sweet.

She pours water into the bowlful of fluffy white clouds, dives in with both hands and pulls her fingers up through the murky liquid. Soft coconut cream runs in rivers to your elbows and you sob, punching at memory, fists on thighs. Kalesi brushes away fury and noise, smoothes away your hair with rough knuckles.

Behind the house, the men tend the fire and pound kava. Soon they will unwrap the banana leaves and bring the food to the porch. Chicken, cassava, taro leaves. Sometimes they throw in Maggi instant noodles. Bury the food and cook it slowly; everything tastes good that way. The small fish boil on the gas burner. They will be eaten, too, down to every small bone. The kids will fight over the succulent eyeballs.

Later you climb into bed with your child, breathe in her sweet salt skin, spy a speck in her whiteblonde hair, then another. You pinch lice between finger and thumb. You will scrub her scalp in the morning.

Family Values
Jonathan Pinnock

The divorce negotiations took longer than either of us had anticipated. The sticking point turned out to be the question of which of us obtained custody of the kids. The problem was that neither of us actually wanted the little bastards. I think we both felt we'd done our bit for the last ten years and it was now time to move on and enjoy life again.

The decision to sell both of them into slavery turned out to be something of a win all round. With the money raised, we paid off both teams of lawyers, and with them and the kids now out of the picture, we realised we were actually quite happy together. The sex was still great and we had more free time than we'd ever imagined possible. I'd like to think that the kids are happier too.

Maybe we'll find out one day.

Blackbird Singing in the Dead of Night

Claire Fuller

I hear the sound in the room above mine – the attic: like someone shaking out damp linen or rattling at the wooden shutters. I leave my bed and go upstairs. The blackbird is still warm in the cup of my hands, its neck broken.

In the morning I bury it in the garden between the roots of the mulberry tree and afterwards take a piece of board up to the attic and nail it over the broken window. I'm pleased with my practicality; that I've managed to do it without asking Peter.

I eat lunch, carry my fork out to the kitchen garden, forget about the bird.

The next night I wake to the sound in the room above mine. Like someone shaking out damp linen or rattling at the wooden shutters, or the beating of a bird's wings. I don't go up.

In the afternoon, when I'm passing the orangery, I see the shape of a man silhouetted outside one of the tall glass doors that overlook the ruined parterre – all the box hedges run wild and thistles growing where once there was lavender. He is standing like Leonardo's Vitruvian Man: legs splayed and arms raised and the image makes me cry out in alarm, but it is only Peter. He opens the door and steps inside. He has a tape-measure in one hand and his clipboard in the other; a pencil stub is tucked behind his ear. He makes no comment about my noise and I think perhaps he didn't hear it through the glass.

'Frances,' he says, as a greeting.

'There are birds in the attic,' I say. 'Perhaps you could take a look?'

'No problem. Did you hear the blackbird in the middle of the night?' he says. 'It was singing in the mulberry tree.'

Hornet's Nest
Sally Burnette

Ruth Jean Queen reached inside and felt up the wall until she found the switch for the porch light. *Yeah, sometimes you gotta flip it up and down a couple times 'fore it'll go back on,* she said. *There.* It buzzed, dim for a second then turned completely on with a loud snap. *Jesus Christ,* her very pregnant daughter Remington said from the stoop, *You bout to give me two heart attacks.*

Ruth Jean grabbed her purse off the table by the door, twisted back around and let the screen door flap closed on its own. Pulled a pack of Virginia Slims and a half-empty flask, engraved, from her bag and a lighter from the breast pocket of her honeydew-coloured housedress. Plopped down next to Rem and the cat's plastic bowl. Already only a few pellets of food left. *Goddamn possums,* Ruth Jean said. Spat onto the fake rock that used to house a spare key and lit a cigarette for both her and Rem.

They watched for minutes as a slug engulfed a mushroom cap in the grass. *Them poisonous?* Ruth Jean said, not really expecting Rem to know. *Who gives a rat's ass,* Rem said, breathing smoke over a crimson geranium in the chipped pot. She picked at the trail of scabs on the inside of her arm. *Don't,* Ruth Jean said, *sass me.* She inhaled. *Bitch,* she added, before ashing her cigarette in the pot. *How long you planning on being here anyway?* she asked. Rem glanced sideways at the thick wooded driveway. *Depends. Figure Emmet'll feel bad soon and come get me,* she said.

Out of her pink and green striped wifebeater stuck Rem's belly, translucent white opal and purple, a kind of counterglow to the swollen moon. *But he'll want money, too,* she said. Ruth Jean faced her. *I ain't giving neither of y'all shit,* she said. Swished the rest of her Kentucky Gentleman around her mouth, a small amount leaking in between her gums and loose dentures. *And I'm serious.*

She swallowed and hopped back up the steps. Felt her blood pressure spike. *Fuck*, she said as she slipped off the porch into the biggest boxwood, right shoulder ripping a papery nest of bald-faced hornets. Ruth Jean screamed and thrashed amidst their incessant stinging.

Rem grabbed Ruth Jean's purse, knocking over and beheading the geranium, and quickly waddled toward the main road. Ruth Jean crawled several feet after her then collapsed. Saw headlights ignite near her mailbox.

At the periphery of the glow hovered a peach-sized luna moth. The soft eyes on its wings blinked back at her: barely visible in the flickering porch light, prostrate to the eventual swarm of night.

The Taste of Sock and Rubber
Cathy Bryant

"Jump!" shout voices. "Jump! Just *do* it!"

They are in front of her, the other children, waiting, expectant, encouraging. And there's an edge of impatience and cruelty, too, of cats waiting for fledglings.

"Come *on*, Gemma! We're all waiting!" said one of the big healthy boys.

But I'm so scared, thought Gemma.

I might die. I am terrified.

A thoughtful parent had cleared the other children off the bouncy castle so that Gemma, too shy to get on it with the careless giggling hordes, could have a go. After all it was her party, her birthday. The other kids were good-natured about it, keen for Gemma to have a fun time, but they wanted her to do it soon, so that they could get back on. These long moments of hesitation felt like selfishness to them.

Gemma could sense this. It had got to the point where they wanted her to do anything at all, bounce confidently or fall weeping on her face, as long as something happened to feed their greed for experience and activity.

I have to do it, thought Gemma miserably, and bent her shaky knees. She leapt gently up, landed and caught the reverberations, but stayed on her feet. More confidently she jumped higher, found a rhythm and started to enjoy the soft floating dance of it. A smile tried itself for size on her face and she could see the other children smile back.

There was something else in the faces, though. They wanted me to fall, thought Gemma. They are disappointed. And she bounced around defiantly.

At a signal from one of the parents the whole troop of children swarmed back onto the bouncy castle, whooping and yelling. Suddenly the floor shifted under Gemma's feet and the world became unstable and unsafe again. She tried a weak jump and fell with a cry, a taste of sock and rubber in her mouth. Don't cry, she thought, don't cry, as she stumbled off the great heaving mass and fastened her new buckle shoes carefully.

And when she is offered lemonade and cake she is quick to give the appropriate response, wear the correct smile. She wishes that she could either fit in or else find a quiet place away from the shrieking children.

"It's your special day," her mother beams.

First published online at Flash Fiction World (now closed).

In the Café
Sherri Turner

He was talking to himself. Or, rather, he was talking to someone who wasn't there.

Every now and then he laughed, or raised his eyebrows, or made some other acknowledgement of a silent comment. When his coffee was finished he stood to leave, leaned forward, whispered into an invisible ear.

The next day he returned and did the same. Every day for a week he was there.

On the last day he looked over to where I stood behind the counter, mouthed 'goodbye' and I never saw him again.

Until today, that is. The café is still here – I suppose it had to be – though it is more egg and chips than coffee and cakes now, not as posh as when I worked here.

He enters and looks around for an empty seat. I call him over to my table and he raises his eyebrows in query.

"Do I know you?" he asks.

"Not yet," I say. I don't try to explain. We have all week for that. Not that I can explain, not really.

He sits down and smiles.

"The chips look good," he says, "but I think I'll have a coffee."

Just as well, as there are no chips on his menu.

He is a good talker, a good listener, too. I kind of understand why he is here, just not how.

When his coffee is finished he leans forward and whispers into my ear.

"Will I see you tomorrow?"

"Yes," I reply.

I ignore the people in the café who think I am talking to myself.

On The Invisibility of the Deaf
Debbie Young

Only when I looked up from stirring my cardboard cup of coffee did I realise the barista had asked me for my loyalty card. From the look on her face, she'd mistaken my lack of response for rudeness. For a moment, I considered telling her that both my ears had just shut down. But that's not the best chat-up line, especially if you can't hear the answer. Instead, I was terribly British, and gave her a bigger tip than usual. I hoped that her smile and my hearing would soon return.

Neither Lemsip nor coffee had been able to shift the worst head cold of my life. With my immune system weakened by my threatened redundancy, this virus had been clawing at my throat and clogging my sinuses for days. Today it had also plugged my ears. Although my head felt like it was closed for repair, I could hardly pull a sickie on the day that the job cuts were due to be announced.

I headed for the office in the kind of silence that usually follows heavy snow. But this was a hot June day, with buses and cars teeming past. The office was also preternaturally quiet, the receptionist ignoring my arrival (no change there), the chirpy start-up tune of my computer edited out of my morning routine by some unseen hand.

Once I'd sat at my desk, Martin came over and emptied my in-tray. Then Sally picked up my telephone and redirected my calls to her extension. Did they think I was too ill to work, or did they know I was for the chop? When I asked them, they ignored me, even when I shouted and waved my arms. My subsequent attention-seeking tap dance beside the water-cooler also went unnoticed. Well, it was a silent tap dance.

When I caught Beth, my PA, looking straight through me, I suddenly realised the truth. I wasn't just deaf. I'd turned invisible.

The caffeine finally kicking in, I quickly realised how I

could make the most of my predicament. Knowing that the MD was in a board meeting, I headed for his office to find the redundancy list. As I'd feared, my name was on it, alongside a measly pay-off figure. Then I headed for the accountant's office and transferred the safe's contents into my invisible pockets.

Leaving the building as silently as I'd arrived, I congratulated myself that I could replicate this undetectable theft for as long as I was invisible, which, even to my feverish brain, was obviously linked to my deafness. All I had to do was avoid driving over humpback bridges or travelling by plane, so that my ears wouldn't pop and restore my hearing.

Only after returning my handkerchief to my pocket did I realise, too late, that blowing my nose might have the same effect.

Flying Ant Day
Judy Darley

I took my role as bait seriously, standing motionless while my classmates drizzled me with honey, jam, powdered sugar. Then I outspread my arms, lifted my face to the sky, exclaimed: 'Come and get it!'

Our school teacher, Mr Wilts, had told us the truth about flying ant day, that it was all about sex, that the ants honed in on wafts of scent that taught them where and how to get it. The plan was that I would draw them in for a pre-romp feast, absorb their secrets, then share my findings with my friends.

At the end of the afternoon, I adopted what I hoped was a knowing air, and refused to speak a word. For a few days, the other kids regarded me with awe.

Then we forgot. For the most part.

But even now, all these years later, whenever I see a man who tempts me to lean close and makes me catch my breath with desire, I think I spot the silver of a flying ant's wing in the corner of my eye.

Marzipan Bride and Groom
Sal Page

No one believes I didn't do it on purpose. I find this hurtful. I loved Shelley. As cousins, we've been more like sisters since we were both plonked down on Nan's rug ages nine and twelve months.

I'm the oldest but Shelley did everything before me. Walking. Talking. Dressing herself. Her bedroom was always tidy, her drawings neat and perfect. She did brilliant cartwheels and forward rolls while I just collapsed in a crumpled heap. But I never, I repeat never, hated her for it. You couldn't hate Shelley. She was lovely. I mean she *is* lovely.

Funny and mischievous. They always said I got her into trouble but it was really the other way around. I never minded getting the blame. Until now.

She was the first to get a boyfriend. Gary. They've been inseparable since they were fifteen. And once they were planning a wedding, everyone kept on at me about being jealous.

'Don't worry, Kerry. It'll be your turn soon.'

'Don't be too down about it, Kez. You'll make a lovely bridesmaid.'

I knew that. I had a beautiful dress. Shelley said pick anything as long as it's green. Plenty of scope there. She wasn't going to force me into something flouncy and meringue-like.

I sat in Auntie Jo's kitchen as she iced the three tiers of cake. She looked at me sympathetically and assured me I'd meet someone nice soon. We just had to make sure Shelley's day was the best it could possibly be.

'Of course.'

This was beginning to annoy me. No, it made me angry. As if I could be jealous of Shelley. I certainly had no desire to find myself stuck living with Gary. I had other fish to fry. Which is weird cos I can't stand fish.

Auntie Jo handed me a block of marzipan and some food

colouring. 'I'm running out of time. You're artistic. Make a bride and groom out of this will you.'

The big day came and flew by in a blur. Until they cut the cake, that is. Gary tried to stop her but Shelley giggled as the knife went straight through the bride and groom. She cried out and crashed to the ground. Then Gary staggered forward, clutching his stomach and groaning.

And now I'm waiting at the hospital, Mum on one side, Auntie Jo on the other. Both blanking me but still keeping me close. I never meant for any of this to happen. Shelley in a coma with the doctors unsure what's wrong and Gary being operated on to remove his appendix.

I'm scared. When I made them, I'd been thinking about the film I saw the night before. I honestly didn't intend to make voodoo dolls or even had a clue that it was possible outside of horror films and the island of Haiti.

At the time I just thought I'd done a good job colouring and moulding the marzipan into a perfect Shelley and Gary.

I Believe in You
Meg Pokrass

You were standing in a Whole Foods parking lot, waving a flyer at shoppers. You looked as though you could not afford to walk into that store. Your clothes were awful, your lips looked dry. You reminded me of a tired, thirsty young dog.

You almost got me to sign up! The way you held out your hand. I was tired of feeling embarrassed shopping as I did, so many supplements, four-hundred-dollar pee.

"Would you like to sponsor a child?" you asked.

I took a brochure. It was made of brown recycled paper.

Your hand was shaking. But your face was elegant. And though your lips were flaky, your hair looked wet and new.

And I felt happy to be who I was that day, to play the role of a person who was able to offer a child some money.

Your eyes were slightly made up. You were probably after a rich guy. I was a rich guy.

"This organization looks like a good bet," I think I said to you, in my rich daddy voice.

"I think it is," you said, with a vulnerable baby lisp.

I looked around to shake your hand again. To ask you out for a drink, but you were gone, you had walked to someone's car.

~ ~

A week later, a poster with a photograph of you standing there as I had seen you in the Whole Foods parking lot, daisies and other inexpensive flowers strewn around the photo. When I asked what happened, a woman said that it was a car accident.

She was handing out fliers. She asked me if I would sponsor a child.

"I have, already," I said.

It was nice of them to memorialize you in the parking lot.

I tried to remember the car you walked to. Someone was calling you over. Maybe they loved you. Your thirsty looking mouth, how it turned down, because I loved you for that mouth, too.

~~

Some time later, tired and floating again, I remembered how my eyes had felt so comfortable attached to yours.

"Angel Dust" someone said. Your photo, next to a scattering of daisies.

But, who knows what is true? Today, I woke up in the same hospital again. A nurse with wet hair was smiling as though I had fallen to earth. And it was as though I had never gone grocery shopping before, or fallen in love.

I woke up just like myself again.

When She Was Good
Safia Moore

First, I rip their heads off and poke out the synthetic blonde hair. A crochet hook works best. I shave off any stubborn wisps with a disposable razor.

No need for full hair transplants since the headscarves cover their scalps, but I use trimmings from my boys' haircuts to create demure fringes, frames for those elfin faces. *There was a little girl who had a little curl, right in the middle of her forehead.* Men love sable hair against milky skin. I should never have told her that.

Barbies are extortionate so my dolls come from the Chinese market. I stitch shimmering sequins onto their ankle-length dresses until my finger ends ache. Then I add jewellery and miniscule drips of henna to tiddly hands. Finally, I trail a pin-sharp kohl pencil around the eyes. They say the devil's in the detail. I hope not.

Every time I add something to a doll, I imagine my daughter, the exotic dancer, stripping something off, flaunting what she ought to conceal. *When she was good, she was very, very good, but when she was bad, she was horrid.* My diligent hands transform hundreds of miniature mannequins, but words and prayers are powerless. Lord, how I miss her. My heart is a boulder, too bulky and dense for my ribcage.

My husband tuts at my work, murmurs, 'Why not sell them?' I say nothing. He cannot fathom a mother's guilt. Pushing myself to work in dwindling daylight with piercing knuckle pain is my punishment. When I go to schools and distribute my gifts, I seek comfort in the little girls' smiles. I long for atonement. Instead, when I hand over the dolls, all I feel is her slipping through my fingers again.

Injuries in Dust
Poppy O'Neill

Many chose hibernation before we did. It was spreading like a virus, people streaming for an exit. Eat a meal, go to sleep, wait. It was a simple way out of the hunger, the not knowing. I kept hoping for longer than most. The city was silent, I tiptoed around, listening to all the heavy breaths—in and out in unison. Lack of noise hums like static electricity.

Why did I decide the time had come for us? Perhaps one of the children laughing, or my baby's fingers around mine. The sense of a last drop of hope, a way to preserve it. I dragged all the blankets onto our mattress and we curled together. All was calm, all was quiet.

Some time later—a year, a moment, a century—the sound of American voices rouses me. My baby has grown into a child in my arms, mumbling in her sleep. I carry her, taking her weight around the flat, along the corridor. My neighbours' doors are unlocked and swing open easily. They are peaceful, steaming up the windows. Great clouds of breath hang near the ceiling.

I pull the curtains back and sunlight streams in. Tramps sleep a blameless, pious sleep on park benches. The grass is green again. I am the first up. Should I break this spell? Or wander, meet the soldiers, claim this city as my own. I am in charge here, turn back.

I wake with a start. A thick layer of dust sits on my body. I can feel its weight, its shifting sands. The children are asleep, knotted around each other. They are coated, white all over, red lips like geisha girls. I get up, the dust cascades to the floor. Out of the window, the city too is covered. Huge banks where the wind has blown it round corners and against doors.

In the distance I hear the roll of tyres. I think back to the last rescue, the last victory. We sang in the street, big lungfuls of joy. A moment to feel the sun, laugh outside our front doors.

I let the curtain fall back over the glass-less window. This room ends like a cliff, gouged out while we slept. But we don't feel the cold. I nestle back in with my children, and wait.

We Can Be Asteroids

F.J. Morris

'You were born an old woman,' that's what my mother always said. 'Let loose, be young, and live a little.' Her laugh blew like bubbles. She was full of air, my mother. Once I caught her trying to float off the roof but I anchored her, kept her feet on the ground.

I was solid, dependable. She was like the British weather. Her unpredictability was a talking point; her deciduous affection, her seasonal care, her overgrown ego. But I was always the same and I was proud of that. My face didn't flush red in May and wilt in November. I was rock-solid, stable, and in my element. Nothing could crack me, nothing could move me. But when I woke up one morning and my hair had turned stone-grey overnight, I'm not going to lie, I was pissed off. I was only twenty-six.

And when my mother talked about her therapy and said 'if it wasn't for your father, my life would have been a breeze.' I wanted to say something. I wanted to say 'But what about me? Were you not glad about me. Your rock?' But instead my teeth fell out and she shouted: 'I can't go out with you looking like that!'

So I got dentures, walked with a stoop, and everything hurt. My eyes were fading. Before the end of the week, I realised that I wasn't just old – I was ancient, a fossil. Layers showed on my face, my skin folding on top of itself like limestone. But my mother's wrinkles had disappeared. She bought a motorbike and trumpeted down the road, and threw up wheelies. And when I asked her about it she said, 'Oh but honey, life shouldn't be wasted on you. You've been dying since you came out of me.'

That was the last time I saw her.

That night, when she didn't come home, I climbed the ladder up to our roof, shedding layers off me as I went. I wanted to float like my mother. I wanted to show her that I could be alive, that I could float higher than her. But as I peered over my shoes to the world beneath me, all I could think of is that rocks, they only fall.

Why had I bothered to be a rock? I thought of how heavy I felt, how it pulled me to the earth, buried me in it. But when I looked up, I saw a piece of the galaxy burn through the night sky, and I remembered that a rock can be more, rocks can also be flaming stars and planets. Rocks can be asteroids hurtling through space. So I opened my eyes and I leapt towards the sky, and I wondered how much of me would make it to Earth, how much of me would burn up . But it didn't matter. I knew I had age on my side.

Purple with a Purpose
Amanda Saint

She just went mad for everything purple, seemingly overnight.

First, she changed her name from Mary-Jane to Lilac. From her former clean-faced beauty she took to wearing Pomegranate Margarita on her lips, Purple with a Purpose on her nails.

Gone were the usual jeans and t-shirts, instead she filled her wardrobe with a rainbow of long violet dresses.

Oil burners in every room scented her space with lavender. She painted every wall in the flat in an array of purple hues.

Breakfast was blueberries. Every other meal featured an aubergine. She sucked on Parma Violets in between.

She danced in the kitchen to a playlist filled with Prince and the New Riders of the Purple Sage. Every now and then some Indigo Swing snuck in.

But it was all just a distraction. From the bruises on her body. The deep purple smudges under her wild eyes.

Little Ghosts
Jan Carson

There are feral children living inside the Dublin Road Cinema. Three of them: small, smaller, smallest of all. They do not have names as such and, having learnt all their speaking from the movies, have come to call themselves Disney and Pixar and Bat Man, (Bat Man being the smallest of the three and the only male). They cannot remember how they arrived here at the Dublin Road Cinema but they do not want to leave. Not today nor any day they can imagine coming after.

At night, when the lights are down, they scuttle from screen to screen, avoiding the ushers and eating popcorn, straight from the floor, in dry handfuls. They only drink Seven-Up. During the day they sleep, curled like pretzels, beneath the folding seats. Their skin is like milk or paper from never having been outside. When they see themselves in the bathroom mirrors, wild-haired and white, they touch their faces and touch the faces of their siblings. They do not pass right through each other. It is a relief to know they are not yet ghosts. Ghosts are things which end badly in every movie they have ever seen.

The Night Life of Wives
Angela Readman

Every night I let strangers into the house when my husband is in bed. I ease the latch open, aware of the click. Lips pursed, I raise a finger and usher people into the hall. I know nothing about anyone, other than their clothes.

One girl is hardly out of her teens. She wears fleecy fabrics and a hat with kitty ears, prepared for cold weather or a sleepover. It could go either way.

Another regular looks like a banker who's lost his briefcase.

Whoever they are, they slip into stocking feet and congregate by the stairs, small flashlights and candles cradled in their hands.

'You can go up now,' I say, 'follow me. Shsh...' They follow me past the still row of their shoes, a line of people all making a hush sound soft as damp fingers putting a candle to rest. Outside the bedroom, we release our whispers and bow our heads.

The air is full of my husband's breathing. We tip toe in adjusting our heartbeats, each person learns to breathe in when he does. Breathe out.

'He looks so calm,' one girl whispers. 'Content,' the banker agrees.

They sit on the floor crossed legged, tea-lights by their knees. They watch the man keep his eyes closed, frozen, aware our slightest move could break something.

Some nights, he turns his head or drapes one arm over the duvet, and we gasp. Others, he flings off the covers, murmurs something we can't understand and returns the silence to us.

'Do you think he was trying to say something?' a woman in satin whispers, her dress is uncertain whether she's on her way to a party or coming back.

'I don't think so. We shouldn't put words into still mouths,' says an overall man, 'He sleeps. That's all we need to know.'

In flickering darkness, we try to understand nothing and allow someone's sleep to wash over us, comforting as a strip of light under a door. I rush no one. It's like dipping into sunlit water when your hands are always cold, one woman admits on the stairs. It's like being accepted, another man claims.

One by one, the visitors leave once they've had their fill. They shake my hand and thank me; some hug me so close I can't move. It is neither night nor true morning. The sky looks like a chalkboard wiped clear of yesterday's words, only the faintest cloud wisps remain. I stand on my doorstep and watch strangers wander along my street in bare feet, until they're out of sight. Rain on their soles, they sidestep splinters of glass on the path. Quietly, I let myself into the house, just about able to finally drift off myself.

National Flash-Fiction Day 2016 Micro-Fiction Competition Winners:

First Place

The Jumper
Anne Patterson

I fell in love with a jumper last Christmas. A wool-nylon-mohair mix picked up after the Christmas do. On the bus home, I slipped it on. Mmm; aftershavy, inky, lagery with a touch of exercise. If it were a scent it would be 'Office Party'. A group email might have led to a request to pop it into internal mail, so I hung on. I kept it in bed; close in winter; further away in summer; like a lover. This Christmas, I'll wear it. Underneath I'll wear nothing. If he asks for his jumper back I'll give it to him.

Second Place

A One-Word Yet Possibly Longer-Than-Necessary Personal Essay Dedicated to My Soon-to-Be Ex-Boyfriend Who Doesn't Believe Me When I Tell Him I Can Write Something This Short That Sums up Everything There Is to Say about Our Relationship, Our Future Together, and His Allegedly Legendary Sexual Organ

Ingrid Jendrzejewski

Ha.

Third Place

Storm
Gemma Govier

First there was the shock of soft raindrops on my cheeks and nose, then cold, damp shoulders, thighs, knees. I felt if I ran I could protect my warm skin. It even rained inside my mouth as I pushed against the wind. Finally, with misted glasses, I am sodden. My socks squelch in my shoes. I slow down my pace.

When you finally said you were leaving, I was calm. It's not being wet, you see, it's the process of getting wet.

Highly Commended Stories

Jessie Learns How To Keep A Secret
Alison Wassell

'She's a secret scribe,' teased Jessie's mother. Fuzzy and mellow from her first wine Jessie took poems from the box under her bed and offered them as a birthday gift. In the morning they lay in a pile beside her egg and soldiers. Jessie's mother kissed the top of her head.

'I liked the one about the old lady best,' she said. This was how Jessie learned that no place is truly secret, nobody to be trusted. The old lady poem had not been among those offered.

Jessie keeps her poems in her head now, where they can't be found.

Illumination
Judi Walsh

It's dark, and the bus is late. In the house opposite, the woman talks with big gestures. The man turns his glass, half a revolution at a time. He shouts and starts to leave. As he brushes past, she folds into her seat like she has a slow puncture. She wipes something from her face: a tear, or spittle perhaps? The bus arrives. "Oi, missy!" the driver shouts, and I flash my card at him, racing upstairs to the back. I just manage to see her, arms extended, mouthing something, no, *singing* something, twirling by herself.

When Words Aren't Enough
Lucy Welch

He was like too many words crammed into a box. He'd come into the cafe every morning for breakfast with all those words tangled together behind his eyes. The P of Pain looping round the S bends in Loss, caught within the sharp angles of the A of Anger. He'd do the crossword and I'd imagine him looking through clues for the key to let the words out. He'd leave it behind, unfinished. One day we worked on it, all the staff, to the last square, and gave it back next morning. That was when he first sang for us.

Christmas
James Watkins

First we dug a hole in the snow. Mama stepped into it naked; we filled snow back in around her feet. She put her arms out and Papa draped tinsel all around while I tied back her hair. We hung a bauble from each nipple and I looked for the fairy to tie to her hairband. I couldn't find it, but attached a small figurine of the Virgin Mary instead.

On Christmas Day, Tom Raye the competition judge declared that ours was certainly the most desirable tree and, according to Papa, had thought so every weeknight for the last month.

Always One
Tracy Fells

There's always one. The nutter on the bus. An old lady, with tight white curls like finger rolls, takes the seat behind you. She starts plaiting your hair. Bit of a cheek, you think. What if your religion prohibits plaits? What if hair plaiting sets off your narcolepsy? Her breath smells sweet like pineapple chunks. You twist round to point out how she needs a licence to *do that, lady!* She moves to another seat, but her fingers still fiddle at the back of your neck. The other passengers shift and stare, as if you're the one.

Notes
Elaine Marie McKay

She placed the first of them where he would see, then turned from the starkness of its expectation. Later, with taciturn understanding, he wrote on the square of paper in uncomplicated letters. DOOR.

In time, the house was a patchwork of butter-coloured spaces that he filled with the concrete of - FRIDGE, CHAIR, TELEPHONE, SANITARY TOWELS.

For him, scouring the chaos of domesticity, stripping it back to its very foundations so that it could be marked with simplicity, became soothing.

In the evenings, he relaxed, sitting close to her amongst their words, stroking her hair, drinking sweet tea from CUPS.

Energy Efficient, Extremely Slim, Easy to Install
Ed Broom

Trap 3 rasps like Hitchens in hospital before I twig that he's pulled the old cough 'n' flush and bounding off the blocks so I slam the bolt and make like Bolt and flick my belt to give him the Six Nations and I'm rinsing when he dead-legs me down on the tinned Ambrosia tiles but I weeble up to double pump his eyes with naturally derived lemon mint hand wash and Haystacks him into the unfavoured middle Armitage Shanks leaving yours truly to dress, wash and claim my rightful appointment with the Dyson Airblade VI. It's a great drier.

Author Information

We don't have enough room in a volume such as this to list a full biography for all of our authors, and anyway, we don't have to when they have all already done the job for us on their blogs and websites.

So, below, please find a list of the places on the World-Wide Web where you can follow up the authors from this anthology (where available). Please read their other work, buy their books, and generally support them. That way they can continue to bring you wonderful stories like the ones you've just read.

Adam Trodd	@A_Trodd
Alison Wassell	alisoninwriterland.blogspot.co.uk
Amanda Saint	www.facebook.com/AmandaSaint.Author
Angela Readman	@angelareadman
Anne E. Weisgerber	anneweisgerber.com
Anne Patterson	@Patterson13Anne
Annie Evett	annieevett.com
Ash Chantler	@AshChantler
Bernard O'Rourke	lastflash.wordpress.com
Beverly C. Lucey	beverlyc-lucey.jimdo.com
Brendan Way	theflashnificents.tumblr.com
Calum Kerr	calumkerr.co.uk
Catherine Edmunds	@cathyedmunds
Catherine McNamara	thedivorcedladyscompaniontoitaly.blogspot.co.uk
Cathy Bryant	cathybryant.co.uk
Charley Karchin	charleykarchin.journoportfolio.com
Chris Stanley	whenonlywordsareleft.wordpress.com
Clare Fuller	www.clairefuller.co.uk
David Cook	www.davewritesfiction.wordpress.com
David Hartley	www.davidhartleywriter.com
Debbi Voisey	www.debbivoisey.co.uk
Debbie Young	authordebbieyoung.com
Diane Simmons	dianesimmons.wix.com/dianesimmons
Damhnait Monaghan	www.damhnaitmonaghan.wordpress.com
Ed Broom	@edbroom
Elaine Marie McKay	@Elaine173Marie
Emily Devane	@DevaneEmily
Fat Roland	fatroland.co.uk
Fiona J. Mackintosh	fiona-midatlantic.blogspot.com
Frankie McMillan	www.anzliterature.com/member/frankie-mcmillan
Freya Morris	www.freyajmorris.com
Gemma Govier	@GGovier

Ian Shine	www.ianshinejournalism.blogspot.com
Ingrid Jendrzejewski	www.ingridj.com
James Watkins	jameswatkins21@hotmail.com
Jan Carson	jancarsonwrites.wordpress.com
Jane Roberts	janeehroberts.wordpress.com
Jeanette Sheppard	@InkLinked
Jennifer Harvey	www.jenharvey.net
Joanna Campbell	joanna-campbell.com
John Holland	www.johnhollandwrites.com
Jon Stubbington	recycledwords.co.uk
Jonathan Pinnock	www.jonathanpinnock.com
Joy Myserscough	JoyMyerscough.com
Jude Higgins	judehiggins.com
Judi Walsh	@judi_walsh
Judy Darley	www.SkyLightrain.com
K M Elkes	www.kmelkes.co.uk
Kaitlyn Johnson	kjohnsonfreelance.com
Kevlin Henney	semantic.net
Laura Huntley	laura-huntley.blogspot.co.uk
Laura Tickle	copperplatedtongues.wordpress.com
Lucy Welch	lucywelch.wix.com/writes
Marie Gethins	@MarieGethins
Martha Gleeson	@MarthaGleeson
Meg Pokrass	megpokrass.com
Michelle Elvy	michelleelvy.com
Nik Perring	nikperring.com
Nina Lindmark Lie	ninalindmarklie@wordpress.com
Nuala Ní Chonchúir	nualanichonchuir.com
Oli Morriss	facebook.com/oli.morriss
Paul McVeigh	paulmcveighwriter.com
Poppy O'Neill	poppyoneill.wordpress.com
Rhoda Greaves	rhodagreaves.wordpress.com
Richard Holt	bigstorysmall.com
Rob Walton	www.linesofdesire.co.uk
Russel Dent	www.rjdent.com
Ruth McKee	@RuthMcKee
Safia Moore	www.topofthetent.com
Sal Page	sal-cobbledtogether.blogspot.co.uk
Sally Burnette	@dunebuggy12
Santino Prinzi	tinoprinzi.wordpress.com
Sarah Hilary	sarah-crawl-space.blogspot.co.uk
Sharon Telfer	@sharontelfer
Sherri Turner	@STurner4077
Tim Stevenson	www.timjstevenson.com
Tracy Fells	tracyfells.blogspot.co.uk/
Virginia Moffat	virginiamoffattwriter.wordpress.com
Vivien Jones	www.vivienjones.info
Zoe Gilbert	mindandlanguage.blogspot.com

Acknowledgements

First, thanks to the judges of the competition: Cathy Bryant, Kevlin Henney, Cathy Lennon, Angela Readman, Tim Stevenson and Rob Walton. The time and energy they put into selecting the stories makes for an excellent and exciting contest.

Thanks also to Nuala Ní Chonchúir for helping me to wade through the positive deluge of anthology submissions. It was no small task, and her practiced eye has helped to make this a truly entrancing anthology.

Thanks to Jon Stubbington for allowing us to borrow his captivating title for the anthology.

And thanks, and still more thanks, to Santino Prinzi, who is the workhorse that makes NFFD run. Without him, there would be none of this.

Personally, my thanks go out to my wife, Kath, for her support, and to all of you for yours. NFFD is a wonderful place to be, so thank you.

- Calum Kerr

Also Available from National Flash-Fiction Day

Landmarks
(NFFD 2015)
Geographical stories that take you places. Authors include: Sarah Hilary, Angela Readman, SJI Holliday, Nik Perring, Michelle Elvy, Tim Stevenson, Jonathan Pinnock, Nuala Ní Chonchúir and Calum Kerr.

Eating My Words
(NFFD 2014)
Stories of the senses. Authors include Michael Marshall Smith, Sarah Hillary, Angela Readman, Calum Kerr, Nuala Ní Chonchúir, Nik Perring, Nigel McLoughlin, Cathy Bryant, Tim Stevenson, Tania Hershman and Jon Pinnock.

Scraps
(NFFD 2013)
Stories inspired by other artworks. Authors include Jenn Ashworth, Cathy Bryant, Vanessa Gebbie, David Hartley, Kevlin Henney, Tania Hershman, Sarah Hilary, Holly Howitt, Calum Kerr, Emma J. Lannie, Stephen McGeagh, Jonathan Pinnock, Dan Powell, Tim Stevenson, and Alison Wells.

Jawbreakers
(NFFD 2012)
One-word titles only! Includes stories from Ian Rankin, Vanessa Gebbie, Jenn Ashworth, Tania Hershman, David Gaffney, Trevor Byrne, Jen Campbell, Jonathan Pinnock, Calum Kerr, Valerie O'Riordan and many more.

Other books from **Gumbo Press**:
www.gumbopress.co.uk

On Cleanliness and Other Stories
by Tim Stevenson
Thirteen stories that journey between the gothic past and the very far future: where a washing machine arrives unannounced to change the course of a life, and the colours at the end of the world are our oldest enemy. Discover why the mushrooms in the cellar bite back, how a little girl's birthday present can have a life of its own, and why, in the wrong hands, imaginary guns can still be very, very dangerous.

28 Far Cries by Marc Nash
This latest collection of flash-fictions from Marc Nash. The stories range from the violence of Happy Hour to armoured pole-dancers, from dying superheroes to synesthesia, and from toxic relationships to warlords to the mythic ponderings of incubi and succubi. Each flash-fiction is crafted with Nash's usual close attention to detail and the nuances of language, to captivate and intrigue.

Rapture and what comes after
by Virginia Moffatt
For every tale of everlasting love... You'll find another full of heartbreak and misery. Where other love stories end with the coming of the light, Virginia Moffatt goes beyond to show the darkness which can exist in even the happiest relationships. These stories are by turns funny, sad, heart-warming and heart-breaking.

The Book of Small Changes
by Tim Stevenson
This collection takes its inspiration from the Chinese I Ching: where the sea mourns for those it has lost, encyclopaedia salesmen weave their accidental magic, and the only true gift for a king is the silence of snow.

Enough by Valerie O'Riordan

Fake mermaids and conjoined twins, Johannes Gutenberg, airplane sex, anti-terrorism agricultural advice, Bluebeard and more. Ten flash-fictions.

Threshold by David Hartley

Threshold explores the surreal and the strange through thirteen flash-fictions which take us from a neighbour's garden, out into space, and even as far as Preston. But which Preston?

Undead at Heart by Calum Kerr

War of the Worlds meets *The Walking Dead* in this novel from Calum Kerr, author of *31* and *Braking Distance*.

The World in a Flash: How to Write Flash-Fiction by Calum Kerr

A guide for beginners and experienced writers alike to give you insight into the world of flash-fiction. Chapters focus on a range of aspects, with exercises for you to try.

The 2014 Flash365 Collections
by Calum Kerr

Apocalypse

It's the end of the world as we know it. Fire is raining from the sky, monsters are rising from the deep, and the human race is caught in the middle.

The Audacious Adventuress

Our intrepid heroine, Lucy Burkhampton, is orphaned and swindled by her evil nemesis, Lord Diehardt. She must seek a way to prove her right to her family's wealth, to defeat her enemy, and more than anything, to stay alive.

The Grandmaster
Unrelated strangers are being murdered in a brutal fashion. Now it's up to crime-scene cleaner Mike Chambers, with the help of the police, to track down the killer and stop the trail of carnage.

Lunch Hour
One office. Many lives. It is that time of day: the time for poorly-filled, pre-packaged sandwiches; the time to run errands you won't have enough time for; the time to fall in love, to kill or be killed, to take advice from an alien. It's the Lunch Hour.

Time
Time. It's running out. It's flying. It's the most precious thing, and yet it never slows, never stops, never waits. In this collection we visit the past, the future, and sometimes a present we no longer recognise. And it's all about time.

In Conversation with Bob and Jim
Bob and Jim have been friends for forty years, but still have plenty to say to each other - usually accompanied by a libation or two. This collections shines a light on an enduring relationship, the ups and downs, and the prospect of oncoming mortality. It is funny and poignant, and entirely told in dialogue.

Saga
One Family. Seven Generations.
Spanning 1865 to 2014, *Saga* follows a single family as it grows and changes. Stories cover war and peace, birth and death, love and loss, are all set against a background of change. More than anything, however, these are stories of people and of family.

Strange is the New Black
Spaceships and aliens, alternative histories and parallel universes, robots, computers, faraway worlds, run-away science and the end of the world; all these and more are the province of science-fiction, and all these and more can be found in this new collection.

The Ultimate Quest

Our heroine Lucy Burkhampton, swindled heiress and traveller through the worlds of literature, is now jumping from genre to genre in search of a mythical figure known only as The Author. Can she reach the real world? Can she escape the deadly clutches of her enemy? Can she finally reclaim her family name?
There's only one way to find out.
Read on...

Christmas

Jeff and Maddie are hosting Christmas this year, for their two boys - Ethan and Jake - for her parents, his father, his brother James and partner Gemma, and for a surprise guest. It's a time of peace and joy, but how long can that last when a family comes together?

Graduation Day

It's Graduation Day, a time for celebration, but for a group of students, their family and their friends, it is going to be a day of terror as the whole ceremony is taken hostage. In the audience sits the target of the terrorists' intentions: Senator Eleanor Thornton. But not far away from her is a man who might just make a difference: former-FBI Agent Jim Sikorski. Can he foil their plans and save the hostages, or will terror rule the day?

Post Apocalypse

Fire fell from the skies, the dead rose from the ground, and aliens watched from orbit as the Great Old Ones enslaved the human race. That was the Apocalypse. This is what happened next. Brandon returns, in thrall, and Todd continues his worship. Jackson finds unconventional ways to fight back, and General Xorle-Jian-Splein takes new control of his mission. The world has ended, but in these 31 flash-fictions, the story continues.

The 2014 Flash365 Anthology

12 Books 365 New Flash-Fictions All in one volume. This book contains: Apocalypse The Audacious Adventuress The Grandmaster Lunch Hour Time In Conversation with Bob and Jim Saga Strange is the New Black The Ultimate Quest Christmas Graduation Day Post Apocalypse 12 books full of tiny stories crossing and mixing genres: crime, science-fiction, horror, stream-of-consciousness, surrealism, comedy, romance, realism, adventure and more. From the end of the world to the start of a life; families being happy and families in trouble; travelling in time and staying in the moment, this volume brings you every kind of story told in every kind of way.

Printed in Great Britain
by Amazon